Richard House is currently the S
Arts at Nottingham Trent Unive
is also published by Serpent's Tai

Praise for *Uninvited*

'House's gifts shine through. With a single observation he can give lasting resonance to a few seconds of human awkwardness . . . When all the elements of the novel finally start working together, *Uninvited* is as powerful as Richard House's bleak, beautiful debut, *Bruiser*' *Times Literary Supplement*

'House's sparse, beautiful text is a literary triumph' *The Big Issue in the North*

'A poignant tragedy of the mundane: London life on the margin in a community of squatters where threats of eviction and urban violence are the stuff of everyday existence' *The Bookseller*

'Dark without being bleak, *Uninvited* is strangely moving, and the mood stays when the book is over' *The List*

'Richard House is a master of words and pulls you along with the characters, for better or worse you feel that if you stop reading you might just miss something . . . I have not been sucked into a book as much as this one for a long long time and it deserves to do well' *Scotsgay Magazine*

'House is a master of flawed character and unexpectedly moving images' *New Statesman*

'In *Uninvited*, Richard House proves that the promise of his earlier novel, *Bruiser*, was not a quirk. It is a privilege to observe this still-blossoming artist exploring the extent of his powers' *Lambda Book Report*

Also by Richard House and published by Serpent's Tail

Bruiser

'Richard House's sad, beautifully crafted novel is a triumph of story telling. His engaging characters leave the reader both astonished and hopeful. Here is an amazing writer.' David Sedaris

'Its dark mood of self-examination, its deathly reticence and its dream-like progression all make for a very intimate and disturbing work of considerable bleak passion. *Bruiser* is the best gay novel I have read this year.' *Independent*

Uninvited

Richard House

Library of Congress Catalog Card Number: 2003105195

A complete catalogue record for this book can be obtained from the British Library on request

First published in 2001 by Serpent's Tail,
4 Blackstock Mews, London N4 2BT
website: www.serpentstail.com

First published in this 5-star edition in 2003

Printed by Mackays of Chatham, plc
10 9 8 7 6 5 4 3 2 1

Thanks to Amy Scholder, Tony Peake, John Ploof, Laura & Seth Harrison, Chris Mundy, Dr Sophie Lycouris, Darren Bourne, David Hughes, and *Liveartmagazine*.

For Pete Bowcott and Nick Webster

7, Hopewell Terrace, SE14

It came again, quieter the second time. Ian leant into the darkness concentrating on the black playing fields, his face close to the window – and there, a third time, came a strained and hollow yelp followed by a brief, pressured cough. There were foxes out on the field, city foxes with thick and ragged coats and slender, dainty legs. He heard them screeching and barking behind the terrace at night, and thought that the sound was lonely. Ian counted between the calls, slowly drawing in his breath. In one hand, slung between his legs, was an empty bottle of flat and soured beer. He had not eaten and he felt sullen and heavy.

Downstairs an argument roiled between Malc and his brother Terry. Their voices weltered through the hall, growing harsher and more insistent as the night wore on.

Ian stared into the darkness at the small faint lights prickling across the fields, certain that the cry was not human.

Terry returned to the terrace mid-morning, and the argument

continued fiercer than the night before. Unsettled by the squabbling, Ian rested on his side, curling his fingers in time to the soft tick of his watch. The circulation to his right arm was poor and he would wake most mornings with cold fingers and a pinch deep in his right shoulder, a ghost of a cramp that would grow steadily throughout the day. The air in the room was still and musty. Sitting up, he used his right foot and left hand to separate his T-shirt and sweater. Still warm, the wool smelled sour.

On the floor beside his mattress was a splint, a slim and hard plastic tongue which attached to his forearm and hand with three Velcro straps. Without it, his hand contracted awkwardly towards his wrist.

Fastening the splint to his right forearm Ian considered which he would rather have, breakfast or cigarettes. Louise owed him for painting the hall and kitchen, and he was short of money, but she was out and would probably not return until the evening.

At the far back edge of the field was a burnt shell of a car in a scorched patch of grass. Closer, down in the yard, two boys waited for Terry. One sat on the steps, dozy and useless, the knuckles on both his hands bandaged with tape. The other, younger still, stood with his back to the house, his hands fidgeting in his pockets. Terry was seldom without a loose group of boys who skulked after him, sometimes by bike, often on foot, waiting to catch his eye to trade small handfuls of sedatives that they had pilfered from local clinics, pharmacies, and parent's medicine cabinets. Terry bartered and traded whatever was available. He never paid and he never accepted money. It wasn't business, he said, it was recreation.

As Ian watched the two boys the squabbling subsided and the house became silent. Adjusting the Velcro straps around his hand and wrist, he wondered if he should leave the house. There was nothing in his room worth taking, a mattress, an unsound chair, bedding and clothes, a hammer and an empty beer bottle; the room itself was nothing but dry linoleum and wallpaper with a faded floral pattern, and dust, an endless quantity of dust that the house shed daily.

Ian returned to the Terrace mid-afternoon to find the front door wide open. Scattered across the hall and stairs were a quantity of pills; soft gelatin capsules with shiny blue casings. Ian stepped carefully through the hall avoiding them. A scuffed and dirty blanket sprawled halfway down the stairs. Too lazy to dress, Malc often wandered about the house with a blanket or a bed-sheet wrapped over his shoulders and around his waist. Uncomfortable with the quiet, Ian called up the stairs, and was surprised to find the house empty.

On the kitchen counter he found two new cans of paint and a note from Louise. Malc has fallen downstairs, the note read. I'm going to the hospital with him. The ambulance crew have contacted the police. Get rid of the pills.

Ian set to work immediately, sweeping the pills together and stowing them in a half-full can of white paint. A pure indigestible blue, dark and beetle-like, there were too many to count. Soft and gummy, they stuck to his hand, staining his fingers an inky black, and leaving a thin blue trace as they dropped into the paint. Talking out loud to reassure himself, he thought that he should recognize them but he did not.

Finding a lid, Ian sealed the can and hid it in a cupboard beneath the sink, behind other tins of paint and turpentine. Closing the cupboard, he thought that he should go straight to the hospital rather than wait for the police.

Louise sat away from the Emergency Room, in a wide green and white corridor with banks of chairs bolted to the floor. Standing up as soon as she saw Ian, she assured him that Malc would be alright. As far as the hospital could tell the pills were similar to his regular medication, anti-convulsants that would chemically calm the brain, and more or less shut it down. The drugs would have no lasting effect, and other than a broken arm and two cracked teeth, nothing appeared to be seriously wrong. But what was he thinking, taking those pills in the first place?

Louise spoke in a low voice. Her throat, she said, was sore, and her voice was beginning to rasp, as it did whenever she was tired or aggravated, and she was tired and aggravated with Malc. Taking off her coat, she folded it over her arms. How idiotic was it that a man who regularly forgets to take his medication, which is supposed to help prevent his seizures, then gives himself a fit taking drugs he isn't supposed to take? How stupid can a person be?

She found him unconscious, she said, sprawled on his stomach halfway down the stairs, wearing only his underpants and looking like a cartoon drunk. As no one else lived on the Terrace, and there was no one around to help, she had run to the telephones on New Cross Road to call an ambulance. While she was out, Malc crawled down the last two steps and along the corridor. By the time the ambulance arrived he was at the kitchen door. It couldn't have happened at a worse time. The council had been very clear, any trouble of any kind and they would lose Hopewell.

'Did the police come to the house?' she asked.

Ian shook his head and they both looked awkwardly at the floor.

Louise folded her arms over her coat. Her hair, unevenly parted, looked darker under the strip lighting, her round face paler. With shadows permanently under her eyes, she always looked tired. It was possible, she said, that the police wouldn't report the incident to the council, but she doubted that they would be so lucky. He didn't have to stay. 'I'll wait until Terry arrives.'

'He won't come. They were arguing again this morning.' Terry lived on Jerningham Road, two streets away from Hopewell. For the next couple of days, he would stay at his own house. This was the pattern between the brothers, fights followed by resentful absences.

Louise shook her head. 'I thought he was dead.' Her voice was flat, matter of fact. 'I thought he'd broken his neck.' She unfolded her arms and looked sideways at Ian. 'You said he wouldn't be any trouble.'

'I said he wouldn't be much trouble.'

A nurse called for Louise and asked if they wanted to sit with Malc before they took him to the ward. The nurse glanced quickly at Ian's arm and splint.

They followed the man through the Emergency Room to a row of curtained cubicles. Drawing back one of the curtains, the nurse said again that they could sit with him.

Dressed in a pair of old underpants, Malc sat upright on a high bed, his knees level to Ian's stomach, and his right arm set in a fresh white cast. Blank, dozy, and faintly ridiculous, with his chin grazed, his lips wet, and his dark lanky hair matted to his forehead, he looked pallid and sickly and thin. Not quite conscious, he stared vacantly at Ian, appearing to frown, his eyes deep pockets under the sharp and crude fluorescent light.

Talking to Ian, the nurse asked about the seizures. How often did they occur? After waiting three hours Louise was now being ignored.

'Big ones? Once a month,' Ian answered. 'Don't you think?' He deferred to Louise.

She agreed. 'But most days he has a small episode of some kind.'

Four years before, while painting gutters on a house in Plaistow, Malc had fallen off a ladder, cracking his head open on the garage roof, and shattering his left arm and hip on the concrete driveway. He left hospital three-and-a-half months later looking drawn and twisted, with bulky joints and a huge shaved head, and nearly one third of his skull replaced with a titanium plate. Not long after the fall he had started having seizures.

Malc's eyes fixed on Ian's face, the pupils blown wide.

'Do you think he can tell what's going on?'

The nurse said no. 'He probably can't even hear you.'

Still focused on Ian, Malc blinked.

Ian stood at his bedroom window rhythmically multiplying numbers in his head. Although he was tired he knew that he would not sleep. The house felt vacant and weightless. Beyond the black hollow of the yard was a solid dark block, a no-man's land between the Terrace and the estate. There were contractors and developers on one side and a broad empty field on the other.

Hopewell Terrace was a cul-de-sac, an unbroken row of six council houses with one separate house, number 7, set at a right angle at the end of the street.

Viewed from the back the houses appeared derelict. The windows were bare, and the small unkempt yards reeked of rot. Looking out into a wide, black sky, Ian counted slowly, juggling the fret and excitement of the day with the urge to tell someone about it. There was only one person he cared to tell. But Gordon would not be home. Ian looked again at Louise's note, re-reading her message. A clear story told in four sentences, typically succinct. The paper was folded into quarters, the seams doubled from being creased first one way and then another. On the reverse, written in Malc's untidy and slanted script, was a list of names:

Michael Alton, Donald Anderson, Malcolm Andrews, Ian Butcher, Robert Clark, Matthew Forest, Lee Gordon, Alan Hudson, David Jones, Andrew King, Terrance Kelman, Robert Latchford, David Lawson, Henry Lewis, Simon McDonald, Duncan McGregor, Jim McKenzie, John Peterson, James Pearson, Steven Seargent, David Smallford, Christopher

Smith, Dennis Taylor, Simon Thomas, David Williams, Peter Wittle, William Young.

Ian read the list several times, repeating the names out loud in a soft supple rhythm.

The sheer mass of people arriving at Charing Cross between half-past eight and nine o'clock meant that Ian could slip through the gate without paying. The fine was £10, a small cost when reckoned against a week of free travel. Ian kept a travel pass with a false name in his wallet in case he was caught. The pass was also used to open utility accounts at new squats. The bills for Hopewell came addressed to a Mr Ian Cullom. Ian kept his work pass and cashcard with his real name in a separate pocket. Most mornings he would walk with Malc to New Cross Gate station, where they would separate, Malc catching a bus, and Ian taking the train.

Ian walked briskly, winding through the concourse ahead of the other commuters, always expecting to be caught. A sweet trace of scorched almonds hung in the air, a homely smell of marzipan and baked pastries. At the exit on to Craven Street, slumped in a wheelchair at the top of the steps, a double amputee begged for loose change. The man wore shorts in spite of the cold. Both legs stopped blunt at his knees, ending in a plump knuckle of calloused skin. As Ian hurried down the steps the man called out to him. Walking faster, Ian held his breath and tucked his chin deep into his chest, telling himself that it was only the man's manner that bothered him.

No matter what time he left Hopewell he was always late, and by the time he reached Parliament Square he would inevitably be running.

Sitting at his desk, Ian waited for his computer to start up. There were no interior walls and the desks were nested together, grouped in stations, one side of the office always brighter than the other. It was, he thought, a distrustful space, with nowhere to hide or sneak to, keeping everyone quiet and at their desks. Ready for him on his keyboard was a docket listing the claims that he was expected to clear by the end of the day.

Gordon called at half-past ten. He was on his way from Leicester to Kettering and running late. It was the first call of the morning and having spent an hour avoiding work, Ian was irritable. The signal broke and stuttered and, asking Gordon to listen, Ian explained that Malc was in hospital. Louise found him in his underpants at the bottom of the stairs surrounded by blue pills, he said, and she wasn't happy.

'If I was Terry I'd stay away from Hopewell for a while.'

Gordon said that he would call Terry and tell him to keep out of her way. 'What,' he asked, 'are you doing later?'

'I was thinking about going to see Malc.'

Gordon asked if he wanted to eat afterwards.

'How about Sharma's?' Louise and Malc were both vegetarian, and since moving into Hopewell Ian rarely ate meat. He wanted Lamb Rogan Josh, pilau rice and a garlic naan, knowing that if Gordon picked up the food, he would also pay for it.

Gordon said he wouldn't get back in London until six, six-thirty, depending on the traffic, and Sharma's was out on the other side of Peckham. He was going to see Shannon, and it would be easier to meet at the Olympia at eight.

'Unless you want to come over later and I'll order a take-away.' Ian said no. Gordon lived in a sub-let on Vicarage Grove in Camberwell. If they ate at the Olympia he would be closer to Hopewell.

After lunch Ian returned to find an inter-departmental envelope weighted with money on his desk. Inside was a large get-well card addressed to Matthew Sumpter, and almost £12 in loose change. It was the second such collection in two weeks. Attached to the card was a thank-you note from Sumpter's mother saying that they appreciated the thoughts, cards, prayers and flowers, but her son could not write to thank them himself. The handwriting was broad and child-like, and the word 'prayers' was over-written twice.

Ian took the card to the photocopier. Malc worked in the same Branch Office as Matthew Sumpter, and although he did not know him, he would be interested, Ian thought, in any new detail related to the assault. In a folder in Ian's desk were a number of reports clipped from the *Evening Standard* and the *South London Press*. On a Friday night, almost three weeks earlier, two thugs shoved the temporary accounts clerk from the open back of a double-decker bus as it approached New Cross Gate station. Without any resistance from the other passengers, the two men were able to lumber the clerk to the back of the bus, and strap his hands with his own belt either side of the upright pole, before kicking his feet off the platform.

The rumour at work was that Sumpter had completely skinned his face, and that he no longer had a nose.

There was a photograph of Sumpter in the *Evening Standard*, bandaged and swollen and unrecognizable. Beside his picture were sketches of his two attackers. The drawings were rough and inadequate, one was given a foolish expression and a round and smudged badger-like head, the other, more wiry and crafty, looked like a weasel. They wore identical black knitted hats. Rush-hour, a bus full of people, Ian thought, and that was the best anyone could come up with.

Counting the beds as he passed them, Ian walked through the ward with his arms folded, holding his breath until he found Malc. It was a relief to find him asleep. Ian was familiar with Queen Mary's Hospital. The tall, bi-coloured halls and wards with their swimming-pool stink and echo made him anxious. His parents had brought him to Queen Mary's for a consultation when he was thirteen. The visit was brief; the surgeon interviewed his parents, looked quickly at his arm, then after reviewing Ian's X-rays advised against surgery, saying that the benefits of this and any further operation would be limited.

Malc slept flat on his back with the bedding tucked tightly around his chest. His hair, black and slicked back, and coupled with thick slugglish lips, broad eyebrows and a slight and lanky body he looked like a puppet. A size four head, with a size two body. All in all, he'd looked a lot worse after less serious falls. Asking the nurse how Malc was today, she briskly answered that he was fine. Bad-tempered, but fine. The only problem was his brother who sat with him the whole day refusing to leave until the late afternoon. Arriving early in the morning, Terry waited in the carpark with his radio turned up, smoking and eyeing the nurses through the staffroom window. The nurses sent a security guard to check on him and then allowed him in early, thinking that they would soon be rid of him, but he stayed the whole day.

Ian left the photocopies of the newspaper articles on the small side cabinet, then left, asking the nurse to say that he was there.

Ian waited for Gordon at the Olympia Café on New Cross Road. The night was cold and a brisk wind cut down the High Street. The owner stood behind the counter with her arms stubbornly crossed watching the condensation bead and run down the glass window. Terry was often rude to her, and as a consequence she had little time for anyone associated with him.

As soon as Ian saw Gordon he felt a familiar comfort, and the muddle of the weekend seemed unimportant. Setting his jacket across the back of his chair, Gordon asked after Malc and Ian said that he was asleep but he looked alright. Battered but alright. The jacket was new and made of a rich brown supple leather, so soft to look at that Ian immediately wanted to touch it. A bulky black zippered wallet, the size of a folded newspaper, was tucked into the inside pocket. Gordon used the wallet to carry a rent-ledger and payment book for his work.

They both ordered the all-day breakfast, and as they waited Ian described Malc's accident and the pills. More than anything else the pills were what bothered Louise.

Gordon said that there was nothing to worry about. In two days Malc would be back at Hopewell and the incident would be forgotten.

'What was the fight about?'

'I couldn't hear properly. They were both drunk and calling each other names. It started at the Britannia with Terry pretending his keys were stuck to Malc's head.'

Changing the subject, Gordon asked if Ian had given any more thought to Easter.

Ian nodded. Last Easter they spent three nights in a twin room above a coffee and dope bar in Amsterdam. The bar opened late in the afternoon and closed at five in the morning. The nights were long and slow and they slept through the days and saw nothing of the city, going downstairs as soon as the bar opened. It was, they agreed, better than Turkey. Better even than Rome two years before. If nothing else came up, they could always return to Amsterdam.

'I don't know how many days I have.'

'Take some sick days.'

Ian shrugged. 'There aren't many sick days on a temporary contract.' It was unlikely that he would be able to afford a holiday without going into debt.

Gordon opened his hands. One place was as good as another. If money was a problem he could help a little. But Amsterdam wouldn't break the bank.

When their meals arrived they each separated the eggs from the baked beans, careful not to puncture the yolks. Gordon waited as Ian cut his food into small manageable bites. Patterson was anxious to have the rents in on time this month, he said, and wouldn't pay for any extra days. Gordon sat upright, stretching, the booth was too narrow for his legs. Having spent the past two days driving round Leicester and Kettering in

Patterson's car, there were still rents to collect in Deptford and Surrey Docks, and he was eager to get the job done. When Terry was working they could manage everything in two days. Now he was on his own he was pushed to get everything done in three. Without Terry people thought that they could hold back on their rents, and they needed to learn that business with Gordon would be no different. Gordon was six foot four barefoot, with a sallow angular face, and Ian could not imagine anyone quibbling or haggling with him for a few extra days.

They ate in silence, not looking up until they were done. Still hungry, Ian sat back and wiped his mouth. Disgusted at the sweaty walls and the brown and sodden ceiling tiles, he kept his eyes on the table. Gordon asked where he disappeared to on Saturday night, and Ian shook his head.

'You didn't go anywhere then?'

Ian looked out at the street and shook his head again, watching the traffic lights fur and spangle across the wet windows. No, he hadn't gone anywhere. He was tired, he said, and a little drunk.

'I went back to Hopewell, finished off the last beer, and listened to the foxes.'

'And?'

'Nothing. I sat listening.' Ian ran his tongue over his lips, tasting salt and grease. He felt indecisive, unsatisfied. 'I think I need a change.'

Gordon patted his pocket, searching for his cigarettes. Finding them, he took out two, and passing one to Ian said that everybody felt the same. A long winter makes everyone restless. That's all it was.

Gordon paid for the breakfasts while Ian waited outside finishing his cigarette. He held the door open for Gordon, watching him push his fists down through his jacket sleeves. For one short moment as the door swung back, reflected light caught in his eyes, and Gordon looked unrecognizable, feral.

*

As Ian walked up the stairs he picked up Malc's blanket. The electricity was off and he remembered that Louise had asked him to buy a new meter card. Pills slipped out from the cloth and spun down into the hall, rattling on the steps. Downstairs, torchlight seeped under Louise's door, catching on the uneven floorboards. Picking up two of the pills, he slipped them into his pocket.

Lit by the dirty ochre spill from the street lamps, Malc's room was littered with newspapers and clothes. An iron-frame bed with two stacked single mattresses was pulled away from the wall, quilt and pillows bundled in the centre. Painted above the bed and across two walls was a cartoon of a tiger pouncing on a plump and terrified pig. The tiger's tail whipped up to the ceiling, its long, sleek body stretched the whole length of the wall. A policeman's helmet toppled off the pig's head as it scurried upright on its hind legs, scrambling toward the door with panic in its eyes and black turds flying from its arse. The painting dominated the small and messy room. Ian folded the blanket and laid it on Malc's bed. The mattress reeked of the light pissy whiff of warm lager.

On the floor by the door was a pack of cigarettes, Marlboro, Terry's brand, one left in the packet. Massaging his arm, Ian thought that he should not be in the room.

Louise came up the stairs, knocked on Ian's door and asked if she could have a word.

Coming out on to the landing, Ian said that he was returning Malc's blanket to his room. Louise stood in the briny darkness at the top of the stairs, her arms folded.

'Have you seen the painting?'

'Of the tiger?' Louise nodded.

'I didn't know he was that good.'

Malc's door closed slowly behind him.

'Did you see him at the hospital tonight?'

Ian said yes, he was asleep but he looked alright.

'The police were here this afternoon.' Louise hooked her

hair behind her ear. 'They want to talk with you. They want you to go to the station tomorrow.'

'I'm working.'

'The incident number and the officer's name are on a card in the kitchen. He said he'd be there at eight.'

Ian did not like being told what to do. 'Have you talked with them?'

Louise nodded. 'They want to know where the pills came from. And there are some questions about the accident. Malc's wrist is broken. Which means he was probably trying to stop himself falling. He wouldn't have held out his arm if it was a seizure. They think his seizure started after the accident.'

Ian shrugged, irritated. 'I don't know any more than you do.'

'There's more to tell you.' Louise stood uncomfortably beside the banisters. The water, gas, and electricity were shut off. The builders were also gone. 'They've finished the other houses and shut everything off. If the builders aren't here I don't see how we can get anything back on this time.'

'We pay our bills. They can't leave us without power.'

'They can do what they like, it's a squat. They don't have to do anything.'

Louise took a step back. 'There's more,' she said. 'I'm moving. I'm leaving Hopewell.' Leaning back against the wall she said that there wasn't any sense in dragging it out. 'If they've finished the other houses that means they're ready to start here. It's only a matter of a month or maybe even a week before they evict us.'

'I thought the council were supposed to let you know what was going on? I thought you had an agreement with them?'

Louise gave a mock groan of frustration. 'Ian. I'm leaving the house. There's a squat off the Green in Islington.' Her voice echoed in the hallway. 'Look at what's happening here.

Malc and Terry use the house as their private pharmacy, the police come and go as they please, and now we don't have any water and no electricity. It's better to move now before we get kicked out.'

Ian looked down the stairs. The disappointment he felt was pragmatic, not sentimental. He had painted the kitchen, the hall, Louise's room, the banisters, and the skirting board throughout the house, everywhere except his and Malc's room, believing that he would at least see out the year in it; and besides, she owed him money.

She was, she said, tired of thinking about it, and there was little point in talking. The decision was made. There was one last load to take. It was ridiculous having so much stuff. Ian could do what he liked with what was left.

Ian called Gordon from the telephones at the bottom of Jerningham Road. Small packets of flowers and messages were tied to the railings by New Cross Gate station, marking the site of Sumpter's assault. It was morbid, he thought, that people would tie flowers to the railings when the man was not dead. Dressed in a quilted coat with the hood drawn tight around her face, a woman waited by the railings. She was there most nights, and Malc believed that this was Sumpter's mother. Ian doubted it, thinking that the woman was there long before the incident. It was her corner. Her place, and something happened to have happened there.

Gordon was not home, and Ian left a message saying that Louise was moving out of the squat and that the police wanted to interview him.

The night was damp, and walking back to the house he could smell the sweet urinous odour of foxes. The streets before Hopewell Terrace were especially ugly; night and day, nothing relieved the compacted rows of glum and stocky houses with their pebble-dashed walls and mottled-glass doors. Coming into the terrace there was a small alley, then a tall brick wall and a broad road, and after, the sudden puritan plainness of the terrace.

Not wanting to sleep, Ian swept through the empty house, compulsively packing and cleaning every room except Malc's. He started slowly, sorting first through his own room. What little he owned, some clothes, a CD player and books, were already safely stored at Gordon's.

He worked through the night, throwing out broken mattresses, mismatched chairs, milkcrates, three-bar heaters, letters and diaries, and uneven stacks of crockery with stains blossoming under the glaze. In a suitcase under the stairs he found an envelope marked 'Noxley 97'. Inside was a hank of auburn hair, and a cat's collar.

Unable to use both arms to lift or carry, he jostled, hoisted, shouldered and shoved the boxes and furniture outside, intending to burn them. He kept nothing that he would not use.

Ian sat opposite the officer in a perfectly square room, at a broad wooden desk. The office doubled as a tea-room with a fridge in the corner and a small microwave stacked on top. The tabletop was sticky with cup rings. A tray sat on the floor behind the door with a kettle and a box of tea-bags, and a small packet of hardened sugar with spoons dug into it. The police, he thought, were even sloppier housekeepers than Malc. The window looked out on to a damp brick wall and blue painted guttering. A small spar of gold tinsel hung over the glass, the remains of a Christmas decoration.

The officer asked if Ian could confirm who lived at 7 Hopewell Terrace. Ian replied that only three people lived in the house; Malc, Louise, and himself. 'Louise has lived in Hopewell for a couple of years. Malc moved in six, perhaps eight weeks ago. I've been there almost nine months.' Louise ran a food co-op on Railton Road. Malc worked at a benefit office on Hastings Road, and Ian worked for the Department of Employment and Education in Westminster.

The officer sat slightly askew to the table, a file of papers set on his lap. He wore a small grey suit. Early morning and his jowls were blue with stubble.

'Did you hear any of the argument between Malc and his brother on the night before the incident?'

Ian said yes. He hadn't heard any particulars, but he could hear them fighting.

'Could you hear what they were fighting about?'

Ian shook his head. 'I was up in my room. They were downstairs in the kitchen.'

'But you could hear them fighting.'

'They were both drunk. It wasn't a fight, it was an argument. I could hear them calling each other names.'

'Anything in particular.'

'Terry calls his brother spazz. If he's drunk he'll say spazz, over and over. It can go on for hours. If he wants to start something, he'll chant other names.'

'Such as?'

'Such as Joe Ninety. Plastic-spastic. Tin-head. Wok-head. Wreckage. If he's being nice or wants something he'll call him Rusty.'

The officer leaned forward. 'Rusty?'

'Malc has a metal plate in his head. Sometimes Terry will pretend something is magnetized to Malc's head, a can, keys, anything metal, just to get a rise out of him. Malc generally uses more normal insults. He calls his brother a prick most of the time.'

'But on Saturday you couldn't hear specifically what the argument was about?'

'No. They were in the kitchen. Terry gives his brother stuff, usually money, insists that he takes it, and then asks for it back a week later saying it was a loan.'

'You didn't talk with Malc about the argument on Saturday night?'

Ian said no.

'You don't talk with your friend after he's had an argument?'

'They argue all the time.'

'And you don't talk about it?'

'No.'

'Has the fighting become worse recently?'

Ian paused to consider. 'No. It's just in our face more since Malc moved in. It might have become worse after Terry's wife left him. I don't remember.'

'When was this?'

Ian shook his head. 'Before Christmas. She left him. I don't know why. She took their son and moved back to her father's. I've never met her. Her father is a property developer. Patterson. Terry did some work for him last year, collecting rents. I think Patterson was sorry to let him go. But he didn't have much of a choice.'

'Because of his daughter?'

'That's what Terry says.'

'You weren't present when the incident occurred?'

Ian shook his head. 'I left the house at about twelve-thirty, one o'clock.'

'Was there anyone other than Malc in the house when you left?'

'No. No-one else. Malc was in his bedroom. I didn't hear Terry leave, but I'm certain he wasn't in the house. Terry doesn't live at Hopewell, but he's around most of the time. Earlier there were two people in the yard. Friends of Terry's. I waited for them to go before I went out. Louise thinks that they've been stealing from us. She's had money taken from her room, and they were the only people who could have taken it.'

'Are you aware that Terrence Noxley has a record of assault?'

Unsettled, Ian shook his head and shifted uncomfortably in

his seat. Carefully watching Ian's face, the officer waited for a response.

'Assault? Who has he assaulted?'

The officer ignored the question.

'Have you ever heard Terry make any kind of a threat to his brother?'

Again, Ian shook his head.

'The pills.'

'The pills?'

'How many were there?'

Ian shrugged. 'There were a few.'

'How many would you say? Two? Ten? Fifty? A hundred?'

'There were about three handfuls. Three or four handfuls. I don't know how many that is.'

'Probably more than a few.'

'Yes. More than a few.'

'Have you ever seen them before?'

'No.'

'What kind of pills were they?'

'I don't know, I haven't seen them before. They were blue, a dark blue. Shiny.'

'Solid or capsules?'

'Capsules.'

'And you've never seen them before?'

'No.'

'Do you have any idea where they came from?'

Ian shook his head. 'I've never seen them before.'

The officer waited.

'You really have no idea?'

'No idea at all.'

'What medication does Malcolm Noxley take?'

'He takes something for his epilepsy, but I wouldn't recognize them. His doctors regularly change his prescription, sometimes he has to take one pill, another time he takes five. Most days he forgets.'

'The pills. Where were they?'

'In the hall. There were a few on the stairs.'

'Were any of them crushed?'

Ian said no. 'Most were dirty from being on the floor.'

'And what did you do with them?'

'I flushed them down the toilet.'

The officer was silent.

'They were on the floor.' Ian shrugged. 'The floor is dirty.'

'Can you tell me how you know the brothers?'

'Through a friend.'

'And how does your friend know them?'

'He also worked for Terry's father-in-law.'

'Can you give me your friend's name?'

'Gordon. I don't know his last name.'

'And how can we find him?'

'He moved recently. I haven't heard from him in a while. With squatting everyone comes and goes.'

'Have you spoken with Terry recently?'

Ian shook his head. 'I saw him at the Britannia on Saturday night, but we didn't talk.'

Thanking him, the officer closed the folder and pushed back his chair.

Suddenly familiar, he asked Ian how he broke his arm.

'I was attacked on my way to a party on the Wellington Estate.'

The policeman tilted his head quizzically, as delicate as a bird.

'It was fancy dress.'

'Did you report this?'

'No, no, no.' Ian tutted softly. 'I say I was mugged on the way to a fancy dress party, and you're supposed to ask me what I was dressed as?'

The officer paused, then asked, 'What were you dressed as?'

'A policeman,' Ian replied.

The man gave a guarded and puzzled smile. Standing up, Ian softly asked why he found it so funny, and for a moment the officer was caught, the smile souring on his face.

Gordon called Ian at work to tell him that the police were evicting Hopewell, bringing with them a construction crew, dogs, and a paddy wagon. He talked fast, his voice garbled by the sound of traffic. Ian asked him to speak louder, clearer, slower, and Gordon became awkward, mistaking Ian's terseness as a sign that he was upset.

'It's happened. Hopewell. The police are closing the squat. They're there right now. Everything is out on the street.'

Across the office one of the temporary clerks started to tell a joke.

Ian drew his chair closer to his desk.

Gordon spoke slowly, repeating himself. 'You are being evicted.'

The cabinet beside Ian was open and inside the door was a ripped sticker as big as a shirt-cuff: Property of Her Majesty's Stationers. Do Not Remove. He listened to the traffic behind Gordon's voice and picked at the sticker. Gordon was talking about Terry. Ian became suddenly irritated; it was nonsense. If Terry knew anything about the eviction, if he knew this was going to happen, then why didn't he collect his brother's things?

'Shall I pick up your stuff?'

'My stuff?'

'Your clothes, and there's a box. They're out on the pavement.'

Ian held on to the receiver after Gordon hung up. He stared blankly out of the window at the bone-white towers of Westminster Abbey. The house was gone sooner than either he or Louise expected and he felt a little ridiculous.

A wasp scuffed across the inside of the window, breaking his concentration. Trapped between the double glazing it spun clockwise. Ian traced his thumb across the window, blotting out the wasp.

Across the office the clerk came to the end of his joke.

The wasp climbed and suddenly fell, its antennae tentatively testing the glass. Ian puzzled at how it could have become trapped. Other black skeletal pieces, fly's wings and legs, dusted the inside of the sill, and he refused to look at them. The glass was tempered to resist a bomb blast. None of the windows in the entire building opened and the office was on the fifth floor. The wasp spun in a corner, curled almost in half, tumbling over itself, stinger extended and beaded with venom, testing for its thorax.

Ian found Gordon at the Britannia. Bunched in his pocket was just enough change for some beers. He would have to borrow money from Gordon to get to work.

The pub was quiet and comfortingly dark; it was still early. Beside the door was a jukebox and a man leaning over it, reading the selection cards. A woman, young, with big tidy hair and a flouncy blouse, stood by a table, cigarette in hand, shouting, 'Percy Sledge, play Percy Sledge'. Ian recognized her from other evenings. It was, she said, her birthday, so why not play what she wanted? Gordon sat in his usual place, a booth facing the doors, with his arms stretched across the back of the seat and his legs stuck out, a newspaper, the *Evening Standard*, out on the table in front of him. When the song started up Gordon folded his arms. Head slung to one side, the woman sang along with a glass and fresh cigarette in hand, swaying slightly as if the air about her were harder, thicker, pressing against her, increasing the sadness of the song. Gordon winced, and nodding at the woman asked if Ian could do him a favour and get her to shut up.

Ian stood over his friend. 'Today was crap,' he said, 'complete and utter crap. I was talking to the police while they were evicting me out of my house. How crap is that?'

'That's fairly crap.'

'Fairly crap is missing a bus. This is crap, pure crap. This is crap crap.'

Gordon patted the seat beside him and asked if Ian wanted a drink.

As Ian sat down his attention was caught by the front page of Gordon's paper. Under the headline banner, 'South London Thugs', were four images taken from the CCTV camera outside New Cross Gate station. Two men with woolly hats sprinted diagonally across New Cross Road. One man, the taller of the two, ran with his hand held out in an emphatic gesture that the cars must stop. The images were grey and indistinct, the faces ghosting so that their profiles superimposed, layered and unreadable, stuttering one over the other. The first image was repeated inside the cover, the figure darkened to a silhouette and cut out so that his arm was raised in a Fascist salute. The cameras were installed to record and deter crime, but in the event they were less than useless. The photographs were so blurred that they recorded little more than a spectral slurry and a time code.

Gordon returned with their beers. Pointing at the picture Ian doubted that their own mothers would recognize them. Gordon turned the paper round. Maybe there was enough there, he said, squinting at the picture. If you knew who they were.

Ian doubted that the attack was random.

'All violence is about profit in some form or other. Profit or hate. Maybe idiocy.'

Gordon picked up his beer and toasting Ian said, 'You're so wise. You should go to college.'

'I'm serious. What other reasons are there?'

'Pleasure? The hell of it.'

'That comes under idiocy.' Ian picked up his beer.

Gordon stretched out across the booth. 'You're not wrong.'

'About what?'

'About profit. Doing it for profit.'

Ian asked what he meant.

'There's a man, he comes here to the Britannia, who'll fix things. If you want something doing, something looking after, he'll arrange it for you.'

'He fixes things? You mean people?'

Gordon nodded.

'For a price. I'll point him out to you.'

'How do you know this?'

'Terry knows him.'

'And how does Terry know him?'

'Just from drinking here. Everybody knows him and everybody knows what he does.'

Ian raised his glass. 'So what's his name?'

'McCarthy. Honest, I'm telling the truth. He does his business here at the Britannia.' Gordon sat upright. 'Anyway. Have you been back to Hopewell?'

Ian shook his head. 'Did you pick up my clothes?'

'They're back at my place. So what were the police after?'

'Terry. Most of the questions were about Terry. Did you know that he has a police record?'

Gordon rubbed his thumb across his brow. 'He's done some stupid things in the past. What does that have to do with Malc's accident?'

'I think they just want to talk with him.' Ian turned to Gordon. 'He was the last person to see Malc before the accident. Have you seen him?'

Gordon thought for a moment. The last time he saw Terry was Saturday night here at the Britannia. 'I don't think anyone's seen him since the accident.'

Ian said it wasn't a surprise, and looking out across the pub he clucked quietly, chicken-like. Gordon asked what he was doing, and Ian said never mind.

Falling into a silence, they watched the bar fill slowly as people came in from work. Ian bought the beer with the last of his money, and Gordon bought the whisky.

By ten o'clock the bar was crowded with students from Queen Mary's, and the older regulars decamped to the lounge bar. Overpowered by the noisy crowd, Ian felt heavy, his body drunk but his mind sober. Gordon asked if he fancied something to eat before they made their way back, and Ian was grateful not to have to ask to stay over. As they left the Britannia, Gordon said that McCarthy was in the lounge bar. The man he was talking about. Ian stopped at the doors and looked back, expecting one man to distinguish himself from the others. But all he saw was a row of regular grey-faced older men, none of them broody or menacing enough to fit his idea of a man who, for a modest fee, would arrange other people's accidents and misfortunes.

Gordon set the guard down on the paraffin heater and sat heavily on the bed, tugging off his shoes. The mix of beer and whisky and the sorry events of the day made them sombre. Ian asked again if Gordon minded him staying. Gordon shrugged, he didn't mind, he said, he was tired and would soon be asleep. Tomorrow he would find the sleeping bag and Ian could have the front room for as long as he liked.

Bloated with beer, Ian stared up at a small pink line wavering on the ceiling above the bed. The room was cold and full of the waxy scent of paraffin. Patting his pillow, Gordon promised that something would crop up. If Louise managed to find somewhere then there must be other places.

'I was nearly done painting. Only my room and Malc's to go.'

'I can't see the point in painting a squat,' Gordon said and yawned.

'Louise was hoping the council would make Hopewell official. She bought the paint and supplies with the profits from the co-op. She still owes me for the work I did.'

Gordon said that he should make sure that he gets paid. It wouldn't leave her short. Louise's money came from her parents. They were both doctors with cosy private practices somewhere down in Surrey. She only needed to ask and they would buy her a house.

They talked slowly, their conversation filled with lazy gaps.

Ian asked if Gordon knew any jokes. When they were younger Gordon would tell jokes late into the night. But Gordon was already asleep. Dropping like a stone into slumber.

All-night trains shuddered past the end of the yard. Gordon slept soundly, comfortably, with his arms slung over the side of the bed, his back a long smooth curve. Jumping on to the covers, the cat nestled behind his knees.

Ian lay flat on his stomach with his arms crossed under him and his eyes closed. Unable to sleep, he counted to himself.

Gordon was out of bed at a quarter to nine, lines pressed into his face from the pillow. Ian rolled into the warm pocket he left behind. The room was unusually cold and it was raining outside. Barely awake, Gordon staggered round the bed gathering his clothes and shoes. Rain streaked the windows and Ian could smell Gordon on the pillow and also the cold reek of mould and damp. The cat jumped off the bed mewing, wanting to be fed.

Ian woke a second time to see Gordon's hand placing a cup of tea on the floor. Set beside the cup was a door key. His eyes itched. The cat was back on the bed sitting close to his face, sharing Gordon's pillow.

'It's late.'

'I know.'

'You should give them a call if you're not going in.' Gordon pushed Ian's head deeper into the pillow and said that he had to go.

Turning on to his side, Ian asked Gordon if he knew what Malc would be doing with a list of names. Gordon stopped in the doorway and asked what did Ian mean, a list of names?

'It's just a list of twenty, twenty-five names.'

Gordon shrugged, and slipping out of the room said that he should ask Malc if it was Malc's list.

Ian's supervisor called him to her desk as soon as he arrived at work, and it was obvious, both to Ian and the rest of the staff, that he was in trouble. There were three dossiers on her desk. Each file sprouting a number of yellow tags. Not having a separate office, Leena held her meetings in a conference room set away from the main body of low nested desks. As soon as they were in the room Leena set the dossiers down side by side on the table, and asked Ian to take a seat.

'Tell me,' she asked, pushing the first dossier towards him. 'How can a training college in Nottingham, a skills workshop in Derby, and a youth training scheme in Stoke-on-Trent have the same bank account and the same finance manager?'

Ian scratched under his splint, guessing that this was a rhetorical question.

Leena ran her eye along Ian's collar, critical and unsympathetic. 'These dossiers have been cleared for payment by you, and they all have the same bank details.'

Opening the first file, Ian checked the pink payment sheet in the front pocket to see his signature. As far as he could tell the claim was complete. He looked quickly through the second dossier. The payment sheet had the exact same details.

Leena nodded, snapping the grip on her biro; click, click, click, three separate dossiers, click, click, for three separate projects, click, click, click. But according to Ian they all used the same bank account in London.

'It's obviously a mistake.'

'Obviously.' Leena looked at the payment sheet.

Ian was embarrassed. He had entered the account details into the computer months ago and forgot to change them on every subsequent dossier.

'Have any payments gone through to this account?'

Leena shook her head. Any account receiving multiple payments was automatically audited. 'You have handled ninety-two dossiers. Forty-eight are currently with Finance. Each one of these dossiers needs to be checked.'

Leena was exasperated. 'Why were you late this morning?'

Ian felt small in Gordon's oversized clothes. He closed his eyes ready to explain himself. She would have taken a training seminar, he thought, on how to manage difficult staff, how to discipline, fire if necessary.

'I had to go to the police station this morning.'

Leena shifted in her seat, unconvinced.

'I live in a housing co-op, and one of my neighbours has been leaving packages on my doorstep. I think I know who it is. Last week I found a shoebox with four dead kittens inside.'

Leena brought her lunch to work in a Tupperware box. Sellotaped to the lid was a postcard of a kitten.

'This morning it was a sandwich.'

Ian tucked up his right sleeve and held out his hands to describe the sandwich. It was in a Tupperware box, he said, pausing deliberately. Left on the doorstep. Inside was a sandwich. A turd sandwich. Someone spread a piece of shit across some bread, put it in a Tupperware box and left it on the front doorstep. Last Wednesday he found a rat. The creature was snipped open, its intestines were uncoiled, and festooned across the step.

Ian stopped and stared at Leena's earrings, focusing hard on the small even clusters of pearls, glossy nubs, as clean and white as chicken gristle.

Leena was appalled and puzzled. Who, she asked, could ever conceive of such a thing?

Ian counted down the hour before he could take a cigarette break. Joining the other clerks in the small smoking room on the first floor, he stood by the window. There were cigarette burns in the blast curtains and unsurprisingly the room stank of stale tobacco. Only the temporary clerks took breaks without bringing files and papers with them, and they stood together in a listless group. There were rumours about Sumpter. In the last month one South London office issued over forty-five payments to one single address. No one could confirm yet which branch was responsible, but few doubted that it would be at Hastings Road which was currently under investigation by the department. If it wasn't for the vigilance of the Royal Mail no one would have known about it until the payments were cashed. Even so, it was a mystery how the fraud was operated. The cheques were made out to the entire Everton football team.

There were also rumours that temporary staff who weren't reaching their quota would be formally warned before the next section meeting.

Ian returned to his desk and typed four letters, describing in each with increasing bluntness that he was quitting. Unable to decide which version to submit, he emailed them all to Leena, then shut down his computer. Leaving his pass beside the keyboard, he quietly left his desk.

Both Gordon and Terry were at the Britannia by the time Ian arrived. Seeing them as soon as he came in, Ian walked first to the bar, a little surprised to see Terry out and about. The pub was busy, more crowded than usual for a week night.

Dressed smarter than usual, Terry looked different. A small man, not unhandsome, he was dressed in black trousers and a soft and pearly blue-green shirt. A new trim shadow of a goatee made his face appear longer and sterner. Over the back of his seat was a new leather jacket, cut the same as Gordon's, but black.

A double line grouped along the length of the bar. Ian noticed with a small shock the policeman who interviewed him that morning. It was hard to spot him clearly through the crowd. As far as Ian could tell, the man was drinking alone. It could not be a coincidence that both Terry and the officer investigating his brother's accident would be drinking at the same pub. The people standing beside the policeman moved away, and taking their place at the bar, Ian looked clearly at the man for the first time, and saw his mistake. It was not the policeman, he was certain, but the men did look alike. Intrigued, he stood next to the man and watched him in a mirror behind the bottles and optics. Both men had short shorn hair, and the same full mouth, similar eyes and noses, similar enough to make them brothers. The man beside him was older and stockier; his hair thinner, lighter, and clipped over his ears so that he had no sideburns; and these small differences made him less handsome than the officer. The longer Ian considered their differences the less alike the men appeared. As he waited to be served the man caught Ian's eye in the mirror and smiled.

'You look a little like someone else,' Ian apologized for staring.

Smiling again, the man said that it was alright. But who, he asked, did he look like?

Ian leaned close to the man's ear to be heard over the music. 'You don't have a brother in the police force do you?'

The man shook his head, and looked at Ian again in the mirror, his eye snagging on Ian's arm.

'Has anyone asked you that before?' Ian ordered his drink, pointing at the beer tap.

The man said that he wasn't local.

Ian paid the barman, and the man asked if he was disappointed not to meet his policeman.

'He's not mine,' Ian said.

It was quieter beside the door, by the jukebox. Gordon and Terry were still talking. Jimmy, Terry complained, was being moved to another school, a place in Chelsea called Foxes Garden. Jimmy's kindergarten was at the top of Pepys Road close by his flat, and Janine didn't want the child anywhere near him. She was turning the child against him and there was nothing he could do about it. Terry smarted as he talked.

Bored, Ian looked up at the small black and white photographs of South Bermondsey and New Cross Gate mounted above the booths. Taken shortly before the war, the photographs showed street after street of terraced houses running back to back either side of the railway lines; all gone except Hopewell, flattened by German bombs. Ian felt that he was being watched. As he looked back at the bar the policeman's double turned away, a slight but definite move.

Terry was out of cigarettes. Gordon pushed his packet across the table, Terry said no, and pushed the packet towards Ian. Only queers, he said, smoked Silk Cut. Standing up, Terry pushed back his chair and counted out his change.

'You'll need four of the small gold shiny ones.' Ian pointed at the one pound coins in Terry's palm.

Closing his hand, Terry told Ian that he was funny, very fucking funny.

Gordon waited for Terry to make his way to the bar. 'Did you go to work?'

Ian nodded. There was trouble today, he said, someone quit their job.

'Maybe they'll extend your contract?'

'Doubtful.' Drinking, Ian spoke over the lip of his glass. 'Has Terry talked with the police yet?'

'He was with them this afternoon.'

'Has he been back to see Malc?'

'Malc doesn't want him there.' Gordon glanced quickly back at the bar. 'I went this afternoon. They're trying him on new medication, which is taking a while to kick in, so he spends most of his time asleep. When he is awake he gets confused. It doesn't take much. He was working on a jigsaw puzzle today. It took him the whole day to work out that there were two puzzles in the box, something that we would have worked out in a couple of minutes.' Looking back at the bar again, Gordon offered Ian a cigarette. 'He comes out tomorrow afternoon.'

'Where will he stay?'

Lighting their cigarettes, Gordon said that they should talk about it later.

Terry sat back down and pointing at Ian's cigarette, said, 'See what I mean.'

Ian sipped his beer wishing that Terry would disappear, fuck off somewhere.

Terry opened his cigarettes, tapping the packet on the table first. 'So. Ian. Tell me. What did you say to the police?'

'Nothing.'

'You must have said something.'

'I don't know why they bothered to talk to me, when they clearly wanted to talk to you.'

'Clearly?'

'Clearly.'

Terry lit his cigarette, and snapped his lighter shut. 'Well somebody must have said something because they were all over me this afternoon.'

'All they wanted to know about was a list of names.' Ian watched for some reaction, but there was nothing to notice.

Terry set his lighter on the table, standing it upright.

'What list?'

'There was a list of names they found with Malc. They wanted to know what it was.'

Terry shook his head. 'Come again?'

'There was a list of names in Malc's pocket when he fell. The police wanted to know what they were. They kept me there for nearly an hour going over them.' Ian looked up trying to remember the names on Malc's list. 'Michael Alton, Donald Anderson, something Clark, Kelman, Lewis. There were about twenty of them.'

Terry cocked his head forward, tongue tipped between his teeth.

'They wanted to know if I recognized any of them.'

'They said nothing to me about any list.'

Ian blew smoke out across the table and took another sip of beer. 'It was definitely Malc's handwriting.'

'Have you told Gordon?'

'What's this?' Gordon leaned closer to Terry.

'The police found a list of names on Malc.'

Gordon looked at Ian. 'You didn't tell me that the police have a list, just Malc.'

Alarmed, Terry turned quickly back to Ian. 'There were two lists?'

'The police had one typed out already. I don't know if they had it before, or if they copied it from Malc's list. They had me compare both lists.'

'That means they already knew the names.' Terry turned back to Gordon.

'What of it?' Gordon held his hands open. 'So what?'

They all sat back. Terry crossed his legs under the table, his foot fidgeting with the table leg. 'Those pills,' he said. 'The ones you threw away. I won't tell you what they were worth.'

Ian shrugged, and stretched out in his chair. 'Terry. I couldn't care less.'

Leaning forward with a malicious smile, Terry repeated Ian's words back to him in a high and effeminate voice.

Ignoring him, Ian looked across at the bar and caught the policeman's eye. The man pursed his lips in a small and guarded smile.

Standing up, the look-a-like took a last sip from his glass, placed it down carefully, and patting his pockets walked to the door with a last cautious look at Ian.

Following after the look-a-like, Ian walked quickly past the toilets and out to the street through the front bar. The man waited beside the entrance to the lounge bar, skulking by the wall. After a brisk hello, Ian asked what he was waiting for.

Embarrassed by Ian's directness, the man said that he was just leaving. Ian asked if he wanted to go somewhere and the man bowed his head.

The options were to either find another pub, Ian said this first, waving his hand to dismiss the idea, go to a club, or go back to his place. There was a private club called The Planter on Bermondsey Road, he remembered, and there were rooms upstairs. Alternatively they didn't have to do anything, but they couldn't stand there. His friends would soon notice that he was gone, and besides, for the man's own good, he would not want to meet them.

Without making a choice, the man asked where they could catch a taxi.

Ian pointed down the road. 'So you aren't a policeman.'

The man said no. He wasn't a policeman. He was a doctor.

Walking together toward New Cross Road the doctor avoided looking at Ian, and he apologized, saying that he felt awkward. Ian agreed, it wasn't difficult to meet men, but he was never comfortable with it. There were saunas set in cellars in the heart of London and out behind Kings Cross. Naked except for a towel about his waist, he could not hide his arm, and at some point someone would stare, more interested in his arm than anything else, and he would have to leave. Clubs were easier, but less certain and always crowded, and the cram and pack of people irritated him. On these nights he felt an unpleasant pressure that something needed to happen, and he always felt separate, distanced by the bustle, the heat, the darkness, and the music.

On either side of the road the trees were shorn of branches and the stumps swelled in club-like growth. There was a car, parked askew with one wheel hitched on to the pavement, the front crushed and rusted. As they had nothing to say, Ian told the doctor that he was fascinated by wrecked cars when he was a child. In fact, he used to collect toy cars and then smash them. It was quite a science, involving a hammer, a pair of pliers, his mother's nail file, sometimes matches, and always, real blood. Nothing more than a small smear across the windscreen or bonnet, but enough to make the wreck as realistic as possible. His parents wanted him to see a counsellor, taking his fascination as a sign that something wasn't right. Looking coolly at Ian's right arm, the doctor asked if he was born with the deformity. Balking at the word, Ian said no and then yes. This was the result of drugs divvied out to his mother when she was pregnant with him.

There were taxis in the High Street, stopped at the bus shelter, engines running softly. The doctor asked if he was still fascinated with accidents, and Ian said no. It wasn't particularly the accident so much as the wreckage, but don't read anything into it.

Ian stood in the doctor's kitchen, sipping whisky as the man showered. A quarter of the bottle gone. Single malt. It was, he thought, a wasted luxury. Except for one glass the sink and drain were empty. Two bills were set square on the counter, side by side. The man's first name was Robert, the same as Ian's brother-in-law, and his last name, Hannes, Ian assumed was Dutch. He subscribed to the *New Statesman*, but the bill was registered to an address on Herne Hill. He drank single malt and black coffee, and his fridge was empty. Catching his reflection in the kitchen window, Ian toasted himself with his empty glass. He looked through the sitting room, listening carefully to make sure that the man was showering. On top of the television was a mini-disc player. The funny thing is, he thought, you would never know that the man was queer. There were no tokens from past lovers, no photographs, no books on the shelves, nothing that revealed a private or an internal life. The only risk or miscalculation in the entire flat was Ian.

Hung between the bedroom and kitchen doors was a shallow glass box with black wooden sides. Inside the frame were three tin shadow puppets. Ian studied the elongated faces, with their doleful and feminine expressions.

These were the only objects of character, hung where they would not often be noticed. There was nothing in the flat that proved that the man was a doctor.

Robert Hannes came out of the bedroom in soft sandals and a dressing-gown. Scratching his head with a foolish and anxious expression, the man seemed lost in his own apartment. The robe was closed with a tidy knot. He asked Ian if he wanted a shower, and then apologized, saying that he did not mean to be rude, he could take a shower if he wanted one, he wasn't suggesting that he needed it. Stepping forward to kiss the man, Ian misjudged the distance and their heads struck with a click. The doctor held his nose, his eyes beginning to water. He looked at his hand, checking for blood as Ian apologized, trying not to laugh. Ian felt a sudden small flush of shame, the only reason he was there was because the man looked like someone else, and he realized that he wanted to leave. Nothing good, he thought, would come of this.

Out of the house Ian felt relieved, and he walked for an hour through South Bromley until he reached Lewisham Way. There was, he argued, little else he could have done. The sky was clear with a full cold moon. There would be foxes out on the playing fields behind Hopewell. The night bus brought him back through Deptford, and he sat close by the doors to avoid the one other passenger who talked drunkenly to himself in a low drawling singsong.

Ian sat in the bath waiting for Gordon to return. Distracting himself, he watched the hairs on his legs describe the flow of water and the run of muscles beneath them.

The cat sat on a chair beside the tub and stared intently at the water, mesmerized by a can rolling between Ian's calves. There were two others, also empty, wedged between the side of the bath and the wall. Ian had opened the cans one after the other and drunk the sweet lager in long draughts, hoping to lose the taste of the doctor's whisky.

He felt stupid for quitting his job, sore for losing the house, but shame, real shame at how he had treated the doctor. He imagined the man confused after he left, possibly angry, and it embarrassed him to think that he might see him again.

Ian slept late. Gordon had not returned, and he guessed that he had spent the night at Shannon's. The house was cold, and wanting to be out before Gordon returned, Ian hurried naked from the bedroom to the bathroom picking up his clothes. The cat followed after him mewing delicately and keeping close to the wall. Laid out across the radiator was a pair of jeans. Emptying the contents of yesterday's trouser pockets into the clean pair, he came across Louise's note and the two blue pills. Sitting on the couch, Ian rolled the pills in his palm, toying with the idea that he should take them.

Hearing the front door open, Ian quickly swallowed one of the pills and returned the other to his pocket.

Gordon was surprised to see him. 'I thought you'd be at work.' Tucked under his arm were two shirts wrapped in cellophane.

'I'm taking a couple of days off sick. I might go and see Karen.'

Gordon tossed the shirts on to the couch. 'Which do you think, black or blue?'

'Blue.'

'You think?' Gordon opened the wrapper. Shannon was working on a show at the Mayfair Regent. It was her first professional job, a proper show with a catwalk, selected guests, the press, and a party later. It was a surprise, he said, she wasn't expecting him. The shirts were from Deptford market and he'd paid a price for them. 'So what happened to you last night?'

Ian sat forward on the couch, pulling on his socks. 'I had enough of Terry, so I walked to Hopewell. Why?'

'We wondered what happened to you.'

'I went back to the terrace.'

'You walked to Hopewell?' Gordon took the pins out of the collar and held the shirt up. 'You didn't do anything else?'

Ian shook his head.

'You'd tell me wouldn't you?'

With deliberate casualness Ian picked up his jeans. 'I wish there was something to tell.'

'They're a bit small.' Gordon stretched his arms out, tightening the shirt over his shoulders. As Ian walked to the bathroom, Gordon threw the black shirt to him. 'Here, it might be more your size.'

Undressing with his back to the mirror, Ian tugged off his T-shirt, and tried on the shirt. He felt nothing from the pill. The shirt was much too big. Fitting easily over his splint, the cuffs hung over his knuckles, but he kept it on. It was clean and starched, and despite its size, he looked smart in it. Through the door he could hear Gordon in his bedroom.

'Why didn't you say anything about the police having that list?'

'What? Malc's list? I thought I did.' Ian smiled at himself in the mirror. Having Gordon believe the same story was a rare bonus. 'Do you think Malc is up to something? Terry didn't look happy.'

Ian opened the door. Gordon waited by the banisters, ready to leave, a sports bag in his hand.

'If Malc and Terry were up to something, you'd tell me wouldn't you?' Ian said, and tucked the shirt into his jeans.

Gordon gave him a small wry smile. 'Didn't we just have this conversation?'

'I thought I'd stumbled onto something then. Where are you going?'

Gordon held up the bag. 'I have to go back to Kettering for

a couple of nights. One of Patterson's houses was broken into on Sunday. They kicked in a panel in the back door – and I have to collect a police report for the insurance claim.' It was, he said, no end of trouble.

Ian held his wrist out for Gordon to button the cuff, wanting to spend some time with him. But Gordon's briskness made it obvious that he had plans for the day that would not wait. As they walked out of the house together, Gordon told Ian not to fritter away all of his days off. Easter was just round the corner.

Ian found Louise in the forecourt of her building. A three-storey block of flats, with small windows and elegant metal pillars, and a yellow brick front. Wearing rubber gloves, she moved sacks of rubbish from the forecourt out onto the street. She was surprised to see him.

'They won't collect the rubbish from the courtyard. God knows how long it's been there.' She grimaced. 'There's maggots. Can you smell them?'

Ian offered to help but Louise said that she was nearly done.

'Nice shirt. Aren't you supposed to be working?'

'That's the question of the day.'

'Why, who else has asked?'

'Gordon. I quit my job but haven't told him yet.'

Louise pulled off her gloves. 'So why tell me?'

Running his eye up the front of the building, Ian shrugged. 'Did you hear about Hopewell?'

Louise said yes. 'I was going to go back and see what they've done. But in the end I didn't see the point. Where are you staying now?'

'Gordon's for the moment. But if you hear of somewhere let me know.'

'Likewise. I've water but no electricity.'

A school bell rang over the wall and the forecourt echoed with the sound of children running, shouts began to fill the air. They both looked at the blank brick wall, listening to the scuttered bounce and punch of a ball that was not there. 'The sound must rebound off the building. They start early. I don't remember being at school that early.'

Ian toyed with the second pill in his pocket. He felt sombre and distant and focused. The noise had a slight physical pulse to it.

'Malc comes out of hospital today or tomorrow. I don't know where he's staying. I went to the police and all they asked about was Terry. I think they were hunting for trouble. Terry has a record. They didn't say exactly what he's done, but he's been had up for assault. Gordon said he knew. Did you know anything?'

'No. But I can't say I'm surprised.'

'Can you remember the note you left when you took Malc to the hospital?'

Louise said that she remembered the paper. 'I couldn't find anything to write on, and it was in his pocket. I'm not sure he knew what was going on.' Louise took off the gloves, and threw them on to the sacks of rubbish.

'It has a list of names on the other side.'

Intrigued, Louise asked if Ian had the note with him. 'This is why you came isn't it?' She handled the paper carefully, touching only the edges between her finger and thumb. She hadn't noticed the names when she wrote the note, but yes, they were familiar.

'Now you're having me on.'

Louise shrugged and handed back the paper. Faintly shaking her head, she said again that some of the names were familiar. 'Why are they all men?' she asked. 'Too many for a football team.'

Ian folded the paper and returned it to his wallet. 'We were at the Britannia last night, and I told Terry that the police had the list.'

'Why would you do that?'

Ian shrugged. 'To wind him up.' He broke into a smile. 'He didn't look happy, in fact it really bothered him.'

Louise asked to look at the note again. There were some letters, she said, about a month ago, that came to Hopewell. They were in official-looking brown envelopes but the address was handwritten. Not knowing the names, she threw them away.

Up above them, distant and grey, an aircraft slipped across a powder-blue sky and disappeared into cloud.

Leaving Louise, Ian took the tube to Covent Garden, and walked to Piccadilly. The pavements were busy with tourists, and the air tasted of grit and petrol. Having nothing better to do, he followed a couple of elderly sightseers down the Haymarket to Pall Mall. The couple strolled without talking, and keeping an eye open for other people to follow, Ian allowed them to saunter ahead, and the gap to lengthen. Returning to the Haymarket, he spotted two schoolgirls in identical brown anoraks. Separating from their class, they hurried away, heading for Trafalgar Square. Ian followed them along St. Martin's Lane and through to Covent Garden, thinking that they might lead him somewhere that he did not know, but it was not as intriguing as he hoped. The schoolgirls kept to the main thoroughfares and familiar places, and there was, he realized, nothing new to discover.

He loitered for an hour against the railings at Piccadilly Circus, watching the traffic and letting the day slip uselessly away. The fountain was sealed behind wooden hoardings, and he couldn't remember if it was a proper fountain or a series of dry scalloped bowls. Turning the second pill over in his pocket, he decided to take it. The first had produced little more than a slight impatience and a stomach cramp.

At four-thirty Ian decided to return home; he would walk to Victoria, take the Brixton bus, and walk down Coldharbour Lane to Gordon's, knowing that Gordon would not be home and that the evening would be as empty as the day. Walking back along Piccadilly he changed his mind, changing direction so suddenly that the people behind him stumbled. Cutting through a short and narrow alley, he decided to catch a bus on Regent Street. Halfway down the alley, in sight of the archway through to Regent Street, he was surprised by the crackle of a radio. Less than ten feet ahead of him, standing in one of the stone alcoves, was a bicycle messenger.

The man leaned back into the wall, smoking, sullen and withdrawn, a bright orange satchel at his feet and his bike resting beside him. The sun shone through the archway, reflecting up from the pavement and burnishing the man's gaunt face and scruffy, unevenly cut black hair. Ian could not tell if the man's eyes were closed or if he was watching his cigarette burn. Turning to see someone else in the alley, the man straightened up and pinched out his cigarette. Slinging his bag over his shoulder he walked his bike out on to Regent Street.

The street was busy with commuters and shoppers, and the messenger walked slowly, resisting the faster flow of the crowd. Preoccupied, he occasionally picked something, a hair perhaps or a strand of tobacco, from his mouth. Ian could see a white support bandage on his right wrist. Ian followed, momentarily dazzled by the clear and cold sunlight, attracted by the messenger's slowness, and intrigued to find someone who looked so languid and so melancholic.

The messenger took his time, and heading across Piccadilly towards Leicester Square, he steered his bike carefully through the crowd, his shoulder bag gently cuffing the small of his back. Ian wondered if the man knew that he was being followed. Other people, he thought, had noticed, and he thought that his arm was drawing attention to him.

Once at the square, the messenger locked his bike to a bench, shifted his satchel to his left shoulder, and wandered into one of the tourist shops beside the Swiss Centre.

Ian hesitated, nervous that the messenger might notice him. If the man challenged him he would have nothing to say. Following the schoolgirls and the elderly couple was nothing more than a distraction, a way to pass the afternoon. The messenger was much more interesting, but Ian could not be certain what, exactly, intrigued him – the man, or the situation?

The shop was over-full, busy with tourists roving listlessly between racks of postcards and T-shirts, blind to the souvenir dolls of London bobbies and beefeaters strung inches above their heads. Next to the entrance was a double row of video games, and the messenger stood beside one of them, his head down as he checked through the change in his pockets. On the screen beside him floated an image of a genie's head. Modelled in flat triangular plains that agitated, unstable, one against the other, the head rolled in a field of blue static; a devilish green face with a white turban, a black goatee, and a thin and vivid red mouth. Its expression was ecstatic; the mouth set in an indefinite smile and the eyes rolled back, unfocused. A printed sign hung on the hood above the screen: 'Fortunes Only. No Games', and scrawled in pen underneath, 'New 50 pence coins. No change. No refunds.'

Ian bought a pack of cigarettes and turning back to the fortune-teller he saw that the messenger was gone. Disappointed, he stepped up to the machine and waited, coin poised over the slot, for the head to turn full circle and face him. As the coin dropped, the genie's head spun to a coarse electronic fanfare, and out through a small slit slipped a small square card:

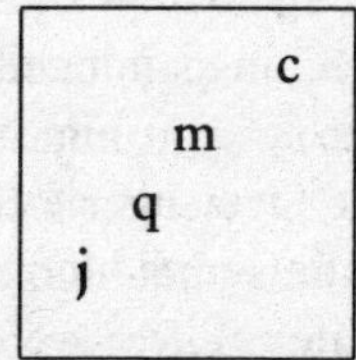

Taking the fortune to the counter, Ian complained. The machine was broken, he wanted his money back. Unconcerned, the clerk shrugged and served the customer behind him. What could he do? Ian said he could repay him his money, but the man chuckled and thrust the card back across the counter asking if he couldn't read. A tiny red light on a security camera blinked over the clerk's shoulder, and as he turned away Ian imagined that somewhere, in a small back room, people were laughing at him. Behind him, to add to his embarrassment, the courier waited in line. Stepping up to the counter, the man asked for change. In his hand was a set of white cards, predictions from the fortune-teller.

Frustrated at squandering his bus fare, Ian sat on a bench beside the messenger's bike and watched him through the doorway, less anxious now about being noticed. Within an hour they would both be elsewhere and it was unlikely, he thought, that he would ever see the man again. He felt nauseous, a little light-headed. He had not eaten a full meal in three days. The only food at Gordon's was a half-packet of spaghetti and a small can of condensed soup. Ian breathed deeply, pushing his fist into his stomach.

Ian woke to find the messenger standing over him. Touching his shoulder, the man asked if he was alright. The question surprised Ian, and he sat upright, embarrassed and a little confused that the man he was following was now suddenly so close to him. The messenger asked again if Ian was unwell, and Ian straightened up, replying bluntly that he was fine.

Pointing at his bike, the courier asked if Ian could move over, and he shuffled along the bench, apologizing. The man crouched beside him, reaching under the armrest to unbuckle his lock. Clamping it into its housing, he stood up and looked back at Piccadilly Circus. Over his shoulder the sky thickened to a deeper blue, and the lights under the Odeon's canopy flickered noticeably brighter. There were birds in the trees, no leaves yet, but many birds replacing them with a sharp, discordant song.

Ready to go, the messenger straightened his bike, and unsure exactly what Ian wanted.

Ian asked him to wait.

Standing up, he searched through his pockets for the fortune. The courier waited, baffled by Ian's request, the bike set between them. Ian found the prediction and flattened it against his chest. He offered the card to the messenger. He paused before accepting. He offered to pay, and Ian refused, asking instead if he could look at the other cards, determined that the man would not leave without some kind of conversation.

The messenger set his bike back against the bench, and finding the predictions in his bag offered them to Ian. Sitting down, Ian shuffled carefully through the cards, counting them. In all there were eighteen. On each one was a variation of one or two sentences, but the words were fractured and their meaning unclear.

Taking out his tobacco and papers the messenger sat beside Ian and rolled himself a cigarette, looking occasionally at Ian's face as he concentrated on the cards.

'They change,' he frowned and his eyes narrowed as he spoke. 'Every other day.' He shook his head and spoke softly. Ian guessed that his accent was Irish, anglicized and softened, but still harsh on the vowels. 'They're all mistakes. Something's wrong with the machine, I like that. It looks like a code.' The words caught in the man's mouth. Awkwardly wiping his nose, he pointed back at the shop and said something that Ian could not hear.

Ian drew out one of the cards. 'In maritime signals,' he said, holding it up, 'SI means "where are you from". There isn't a QJ, but JQ stands for "have you any mail for me".'

Ian looked up, remembering the codes that he and Gordon would signal from one back bedroom to another, flashing torchlight across ten yards of garden. A whole blunt and private language. He sorted through the cards, reading out loud the ones that could be read as code 'YL: "I want immediate medical assistance". GO: "you are within reach of guns". YF: "mutiny". CX: "I cannot assist, do the best you can for yourself". What are your initials?'

'P. F.'

Ian shook his head. There were no codes for PF or FP.

'I knew them all when I was younger. I must have found them in a comic, I don't remember. A friend and I learned Morse code and we used the signals so my sister and parents couldn't understand what we were talking about.'

The messenger nodded, offering Ian his tobacco. 'I have three sisters,' he said, 'and the oldest, Jennah, refused to talk to me. I was away at school and when I came home she ignored me.'

'For how long?'

'Nearly a year. A whole summer and part of a Christmas holiday.'

Ian drew out his cigarettes. 'Does she remember it?'

The messenger shook his head. 'She likes to think of herself as the perfect sister. She wouldn't be happy that I've told someone else. I've no idea why she did it. She invented her own language. Tongue clicking copied from a tribe she saw in a *National Geographic* special. She started a club, her and some other girls. My other sisters were too sensible to join. They had to stand on one leg and point at the person they were talking to.'

'My sister stopped talking to me once. She had a couple of gerbils and I thought they could speak. I thought that when I was out of the room or asleep they would talk to each other in perfect English. But as soon as I was back in the room, or awake, they'd stop. So I decided to force it out of one of them, squeeze it until it begged me to stop.'

'What happened?'

'My sister came into the room for something. A complete

coincidence. I think I realized that it was a stupid thing to do by the time she walked in. But I had to try it out.'

'How old were you?'

'Older than you'd think.'

'That's a strange story to tell someone.'

Ian nodded. 'Actually it's not true. She did have gerbils, and I did think they could talk, and we regularly tried to kill each other.'

'But you didn't strangle her pet.'

'Wanted to.' Ian was surprised by how easy it was to talk. 'My friend Gordon used to talk to his dog as if it understood every word he said. But it was old and deaf, deaf, and was run over in the end by a car it didn't hear coming.'

'No? That's not true either?' The messenger shook his head.

Ian shrugged. 'Serious. It was a Pointer.' He asked what the P stood for in PF.

'Peter.'

'Peter.' Ian repeated and nodded, and when Peter asked his name he thought for a moment. He could give any name he wanted. 'Ian.'

'You don't sound very certain.'

'It's definitely Ian.'

Searching through his pockets for a lighter, Peter stretched out his legs, and with his hand deep in his pocket and his sleeve shunted up his forearm Ian could see more of the bandage.

Ian deftly removed a cigarette from his packet with one hand. Peter watched without offering to help, and Ian accepted a light, cupping his hand around the messenger's.

'Can you think of any reason why someone would keep a list of names?'

Peter looked out across the square, considering the question. 'Of people? Maybe some kind of sport, or a reunion? Why? What kind of names?'

Ian showed Peter the piece of paper.

'Small writing.'

'It's someone I live with. I found it a couple of days ago.'

'Why don't you ask them?'

Peter drew hard on his cigarette. They both exhaled at the same time, and Ian felt that there was a kind of confidence between them. Above them starlings blustered from the trees, flicking as a body from one side of the square to another. Pointing at the bandage on Peter's wrist, Ian asked what had happened. Drawing down his sleeve, Peter pointed towards Soho, and explained that yesterday a man fell down some stairs on top of him. He described the accident as a set of stupid coincidences. It was a cartoon, he said. Just like a cartoon. 'I should have let him fall. It's the second time I've injured the same wrist.'

Ian watched the cigarette smoke twist back over Peter's fingers and catch in the hairs on the back of his hand. He asked Peter where he worked.

'Western Messengers. On Endell Street.'

'What's the pay?'

'It depends. Generally three-seventy to four-fifty.'

'An hour?'

Peter smiled as he replied. 'No. A week. Four hundred pounds a week, on average, and no tax.'

Ian asked if the company were looking for new riders, and Peter squinted at his cigarette.

'Are you looking for work?'

Ian nodded.

'Have you done any courier work before?'

Ian said no and looked at the messenger's bike. Custom-built with a slick silver frame and short stubby handlebars and thick tyres, it was handsome, clean, well-oiled, and clearly well cared for.

He waited for the messenger to ask him about his arm, and when no question came, he held out his right arm and explained that he had made the splint himself so that he could work the gears and brakes on his bike. His hand was weak and most days he could not sustain enough of a grip to tie a shoelace, but with the splint he could use his entire arm and pull from his shoulder.

The messenger nodded and they sat together a while longer. Returning his cigarettes to his shirt pocket, Ian said that he should go. Peter reached into his bag for a biro and a small scrolled wad of paper.

'People are always leaving. I'll give you the number and I'll talk to Dom and see if he's looking for anyone. When you call, ask for Dom, and tell him that you've done it before. I'll tell him that I know you.' Peter wrote down the number. 'You can call any day. But Monday is probably the best.'

The messenger handed Ian the paper, then held out his left hand, and as they shook, they nodded courteously to each other.

Ian rose at noon. Unsure of how he would fill the day, he sat with the cat and spent the afternoon watching cartoons. He cleaned the kitchen cupboards, throwing out bags of fermenting potatoes and carrots. Concerned that he was overstaying his welcome, he hoped that the gesture would please Gordon.

Uneasy at losing the day, Ian began to sort through the jumble of clothes that Gordon had rescued from Hopewell. There was little that he cared to keep. The cat settled at his feet, watching as he picked through the clothes.

The last item was a box containing letters from the council and minutes from meetings. The minutes were underscored with notes written in Louise's meticulous small handwriting. Ever hopeful of turning the Terrace into a legal and registered housing co-op, Louise had met and talked and negotiated with the council over the two years that she lived there, and for a while secured a limited tenancy. Ian read through the papers unable to see what she kept faith with; none of the letters contained any suggestion that Hopewell would become legal, and the language was often threatening.

That evening Ian walked from Camberwell to New Cross Gate, following the back streets.

He looked at the High Street without affection. Either side of the Olympia were two pubs he wouldn't set foot in, a nightclub he didn't like to walk past even during the day, and a Barclays Bank he never used. On the corner of Branksome Road there was a stonemason's, with two headstones in the window, names already carved and gilded – Simon Thomas, Henry Lewis. At night the street held an apt pallor and silence. The shops he did use (the off-licence and a greengrocer's secured behind an iron gate), he didn't care for. He had spent almost a year running errands for cigarettes or milk, and still no one recognized him.

Ian walked briskly down Hopewell Terrace but could not look up. The police and work crew were gone, and the street was speckled with a fine plaster-like dust. Bolted to the side of the first house was a new sign: Refurbishment. Dowling Construction/Lewisham Council. Partners in Community. Under the broad black letters was a simple design of an ample white hand shaking a smaller brown hand. Looking up, he immediately felt relieved. Except for the fresh raw plywood board shuttering the door and lower windows, the house appeared untouched. As he walked towards it he noticed that the blunt little wall at the front was also gone. The house stood defiant, a strong brick square in a welted flat of dirt.

Stepping cautiously through the mud, Ian walked through to the back yard, worried that there might be a night watchman, or worse, a guard dog. The fencing was gone, sawn down, and sections of it were stacked against the kitchen wall. The yard was matted with splinters of dark rotten wood and fist-sized hanks of plaster. The windows on the ground floor were boarded except for the small square window to the downstairs toilet. Ian knew that it was too small to climb through, but large enough at least to see inside.

He hauled himself up to the windowsill, his right arm pushing uncomfortably into his chest, grit digging into his skin. The entire window, glass and frame, were gone, and instead of finding a familiar closet-like room with slick pea-green walls he found a black airy hole. An acidic yellow from the street lamps swelled around the sides of the boarded windows, and it took him a while, even after his eyes had adjusted, to understand that he was looking straight through the house – from one side clear through to the other. The house was gutted. In four working days the builders had methodically stripped the place, leaving nothing but the roof, the rafters, and the supporting walls. Everything that made the house habitable was gone. Squinting hard into the darkness, he began to discern squares of wallpaper, an indication of which room was which, and up high, sprawled across the far upper wall, Malc's tiger pounced into nothing.

Arm aching, Ian jumped down and stumbled back into the yard to look again at the debris. He spat into the dirt and looked back through the alley at the other houses on the Terrace, his cheeks burning slap-red. This was a peculiarly human endeavour. Nothing in nature would be so tidy, so organized, or so deliberate.

38, Paradise Close, Chatham

Ian sat with his sister on the steps of her house, looking out towards the docks at the backs of other houses, watching seagulls chase each other off the roofs, cawing with baby-like cries. The faint and gassy smell of the sea, salt, and dredged mud blew between the pebble-dashed houses. All that could be seen of the harbour were small edges, bright and flat banks of water clipped between the sides of houses and the tops of cranes. The view, like much of what passed between Ian and his sister, wasn't so much hidden as obscured, half-seen and supposed. Karen asked him 'whatever happened to so-and-so?', doggedly running through everyone she could remember that they would both know (Andrews, Butcher, Taylor, those two brothers on Halsey), while her two children played at their feet, half-naked on a cold afternoon, scrambling in the damp scrubby grass. Cloe bent forward on her hands and knees, indifferently screwing her finger into the dirt. Damien, Cloe's twin, watched over her shoulder, staring blankly at the ground. As Ian watched the boy their eyes met, but the child's eyes were dull, emotionless. He tried to remember what he and his sister were like at that age, but nothing definite came to mind.

Karen asked when he was planning on visiting their father. Ian replied that it wasn't going to happen any day soon.

She nodded and hugged her tea, not really listening. Her eyes were hollow, the skin around them dark and dry. She looked exhausted.

'I was there last weekend.' She paused deliberately. 'He was wondering when he'd hear from you. Perhaps Easter.'

Cloe held her hands up to her mother, her eyes broad and trusting, and Karen waggled her cigarette and asked if Ian wouldn't mind taking her inside. Ash tumbled on to the concrete path and rolled into the grass. All four of them watched. Such a small thing, he thought, for so much attention.

Ian took Cloe into the bathroom, and pulling down her pants he lifted her awkwardly on to the toilet, making a noise like a rocket. His voice sounded big in the small room, commanding. Cloe settled back and sat with her head in her hands, and an expectant look on her face. She has the wide fat knees of an old woman, he thought. Ian shifted into the doorway and looked away. On the opposite wall hung a photograph of his parents. So much of parenting seemed inappropriate, spying, chiding, restricting, but without it the house was a booby-trap. That morning they found Damien with his head lodged under the couch, his whole head pinched between the couch and the carpet. Lying immobile and face-down, he didn't make a sound until the couch was lifted off him, then he cried, his forehead rashed red from the carpet-pile. Lifting him up, Karen said that he was a lot like Ian, and Ian resented the comment.

Cloe squealed and called him back. She reached out her hands and locked them around the backs of his knees, leaning her head against his legs. Ian felt uneasy, and one day his sister would too. He'd tell her that he's queer and she would remember this, and feel sick about trusting her children with him. He could see it coming.

Ian sat on the path tinkering with his bike as Karen set up the crockery from the night before. The kitchen radio was on, and Karen's voice could be heard out in the garden, faint, shy and breathy, like a little girl's.

His bike was in good condition, a thick and heavy Peugeot with a dull silver frame and only three speeds. Bought second-hand from an advert in the paper, he rode it from London to his sister's in less than one day after he had moved into Hopewell.

Karen asked if he needed anything washed for work. Ian hadn't told her that he had quit his job. Like Gordon, she did not approve of him cycling. It would be easier not to tell her rather than suffer her misgivings on the matter. Karen disapproved of Ian's squatting, as she disagreed with his decision to move to London, believing for no good reason that Gordon was an irresponsible and untrustworthy influence. Her coolness towards Gordon was long-standing, and she would not warm to him. He was always welcome, she would say, whenever he wants to visit. But no matter how many Christmases and holidays Gordon spent with them as children, she would never specifically invite him.

Ian came in to clean his hand. Rob was still in bed. He was working later and longer hours, Karen explained, as they wanted to buy a house of their own. In a year they would have the option to buy their house from the council, except it was falling down around their ears and what kind of a fool would buy a slum? Rob was the only one with a steady job, on the whole street, she said, and people would not talk to her.

'There's plenty of work out there. Just as long as you're flexible.'

Two years ago Rob was at Karen's side when she was having the twins. Cloe was born two hours after her brother, a little jaundiced. Rob arrived late at the delivery room, and said that she came out looking like a ball of shite, and when he saw all the mess, all of the stuff that came out with his daughter, he thought of Karen as being dirty, unclean. His own wife. This nasty little tale was told on New Year's Eve, after a long day of beer, Scotch chasers, and perfumey champagne, right at the sink. Ian couldn't understand why he would tell that to anyone, least of all to his brother-in-law.

Karen turned up the radio and began to sing more boldly than before. Ian watched the stairs, waiting for Rob to appear. Sleeves rolled up, her hands deep in the sink, Karen looked out over the estate, lost in the song, knowing full well that she would wake Rob, and that there would be a fight.

Just before bed Karen brought out a photo album she had found at their father's. Ian recognized it, a wedding gift to his parents from friends that they had long since lost contact with. Karen insisted that the book was only borrowed, but he doubted that it would be returned.

He didn't want to look, but Karen sat beside him and set the book on his lap. As children they often looked at the album. The hard lacquered cover studded with mother of pearl was so heavy, he remembered, that it would imprint itself on his thigh. As a child he thought it was pretty.

The pictures were familiar, page after page of the same people configured beside a pool somewhere, a Nissen-hut, an airfield, photographs taken before his parents were married.

There were more men than women, all young, clean-cut and in uniform. Ian looked at them for other information, for the palm trees behind the perimeter fences, and the rice-fields divided by raised dirt roads, and the large fecund blooms occasionally, incongruously, set in his mother's hands or hair.

Tucked between the last page and the hard-backed cover were four loose photographs, studio shots of his mother leaning against a plain white wall. Pictures taken and printed by his father. In the earlier photos his mother shied away from the camera, standing at the back of a group of friends, her expression anxiously tolerant, wanting the moment to be over; a face Ian could imagine falling into a real smile once the picture was taken. She was never comfortable in front of a camera, but in the last four photographs there was no uncertainty, and it was hard to recognize the manicured and composed woman in them as his mother.

Karen had collected almost every photograph of her. The most prominent one, in a heavy silver frame on top of the television, showed her standing on a doorstep wearing a long purple evening dress. Taken in the middle of the day, during her lunch break from the bakery, she had to change back into her regular clothes and hurry to work as soon as the picture was taken. One of her doctors, Dr Manning, said take a picture of yourself, get your hair done, make yourself look nice, and keep it in your purse. She felt stupid doing it, though she did look nice. Nice on the outside. Ian remembered laughing at her when she had it taken, but none of them knew what it was for. He could barely stand to look at it now. The day before the surgery, after packing a small overnight bag for herself, she finally told them what was happening. Dr Manning had survived cancer himself, years before, and his example gave them hope. As far as Ian knew Dr Manning was still alive.

Using a public telephone out on the estate, Ian tried calling Gordon before leaving.

The telephone boxes were set along one edge of a grass triangle; out of six phones only one worked. Houses faced the green on all sides, and one of the upper windows was blackened with smoke, the glass and curtains gone. From the clutter in the downstairs window it was obvious that the house was still occupied.

Gordon was not answering his mobile and was not at home.

His voice on the answering machine was stretched to a thin and feeble warble. Ian didn't see the sense in leaving a message.

After some deliberation he called Western Messengers. Peter had recommended that he call on a Monday. An answering machine clicked on, but before the message played fully through, the phone was picked up and Ian was curtly asked what he wanted. Stammering, he clumsily explained that he was a friend of Peter's and that he was interested in becoming a messenger. The man asked if he'd done this kind of work before and Ian stupidly said no.

He was put on hold. He should, he thought, have practised what he wanted to say. After a short wait the man returned sounding a little less gruff. If Peter had honestly recommended him then he would talk it over with someone else. Ian should call back on Tuesday morning.

'Ask for Dom. D. O. M. M as in monkey.'

Ian gave him his name and Gordon's number, doubting that he would hear from them.

Ian took the seven o'clock train back to Waterloo, leaving as Karen was making Rob's supper, although he was not home.

It was a relief to be on the train. He had stayed long enough to have an early supper: tea, sandwiches, and a shop-bought sponge cake with the custard still frozen in the centre. Looking around the room he had felt sickened by the familiar details. The photos, the brass knickknacks, the teapot, even the plates they were eating off, were pilfered by his sister from their father's, in an attempt to build a new home out of the debris of another. Ian ate with difficulty as he was not hungry, despite a feeling in his stomach that was something like hunger. Karen hurried from the kitchen to the lounge with more food, more sandwiches, more cake, promising that the next time Ian visited Rob would take some time off, and they would do something together with the kids. More than anything else this promise of an absent family caught in Ian's throat, and pretending to have swallowed something wrong, he hurried to the bathroom and swept cold water over his face, imagining himself out of the house.

There was only one other person in the carriage. A youth in hiking shorts, with a canvas knapsack. Ian thought that he looked German. Polish. Scandinavian. Blond anyway. Blond hair, blond eyebrows, white skin, blue eyes. His mouth was broad and straight, the kind of mouth that Ian found handsome. It was difficult not to stare.

Twenty minutes from London and still in the countryside, a fox darted out from under the embankment. Running along the side of a ploughed field, it stopped and looked back up at the train, no larger than a small dog, its coat burned a bright ginger in the late afternoon sun. Ian was so startled that he pointed. The other passenger looked out of the window without interest, and then back at Ian's arm.

Endell Street, WC2

It was obvious that Gordon was not home. The house was dark, and the post lay inside the door; Gordon's dole cheque and hefty rolls of coupons. The cat hurried down the stairs even before lan's key was out of the lock, greeting him with one long and sorrowful yowl. Weaving between his feet, she followed him as he hoisted the bike onto his left shoulder and carried it to the landing.

Ian walked through the house, talking to himself as he checked the rooms uneasy at the silence. The answering machine was blinking. There were six messages. As he sat down to listen the cat jumped onto his lap and began to knead at his stomach. Her dry food was scattered across the kitchen and hall.

Four of the messages were for Gordon, the first from Shannon to say that she was working at The Max-Factory on Saturday and Monday nights, the second from Terry asking if Gordon knew where Malc was, and two from himself. The fifth message was from Western Messengers asking if Ian could start work on Tuesday morning. The man had spoken to Peter, and Peter was happy to vouch for him. Come in Tuesday, nine o'clock, the man said, and we'll take it from there.

Ian massaged his hand and looked back through the banisters at his bike, suddenly nervous, wondering how he would manage with his arm.

The last message was from Gordon. A distant voice corrupted by static saying that he would catch him later.

The dispatch office for Western Messengers was on Endell Street, just off the long soft curve of Shaftesbury Avenue into High Holborn. As the message had said, the basement office was reached through an unmarked navy blue door set between a travel agency and a Methodist Hall. Ian stood in the street lost for what to do. Early and thirsty, he was uncertain about the job. Closer to Covent Garden the street was closed for tourists and shoppers. Hanging above the shop and café windows were baskets of flowers just recently watered.

Chained one to another round a bollard in front of the Methodist Hall, the bikes took up much of the pavement. The majority of them were small and sturdy off-road models stripped down to wheels, frame, pedals, gears, brakes, seat; two of the five were hand-painted. Secured by itself to a separate post was Peter's bike, waxed and polished, clean but not new.

It occurred to Ian that he could easily leave. He could call and make a reasonable excuse so that Peter would not be embarrassed. Gordon would take a poor view of him working as a messenger.

While considering whether he should leave or stay he noticed Peter on the opposite side of the road, walking with a distinctive long, almost loping stride, concentrating on carrying two Styrofoam cups. Without his satchel, and with the bandage gone from his arm, he appeared more ordinary than Ian remembered. As he watched Peter cross the road Ian wondered why the man had vouched for him. They had talked for less than ten minutes, smoked one cigarette together, and for no good reason Peter was willing to secure him a job. One day, he reasoned, pushing his fingers between his forearm and the plastic splint, I'll give it one day, and if I'm shite or I don't like it, then I won't come back.

Peter was almost at the door when he noticed Ian. Balancing both cups in one hand, he cocked his head and said hello, but didn't appear much surprised to see him. The sides of the cups were streaked with black coffee and his fingers were wet. Ian caught the door for him and they walked down the stairs together.

By nine o'clock most of the messengers were waiting in the small cramped basement room. Ian sat beside a desk waiting for Dom, the dispatcher and owner, to tell him what to do. Peter sat at the back of the office with his head down reading a bike magazine, the two small coffee cups stacked one inside the other between his feet.

The office was nothing more than a small and grubby den with such a low ceiling that everyone walked with a stoop. With a steep wood-railed staircase at one end and a desk at the other, the furniture was set flush to the walls to conserve space. Under the stairs hung a grey army blanket nailed to a door frame as a curtain, and Ian wondered what was behind it. The room reeked of cigarettes and dust and of musty unwashed clothes.

Dom's desk faced a large survey map of London. The postal districts were outlined in red, and at the centre of the map, above Covent Garden, the paper was worn through in a hole just larger than a fingerprint. On the opposite wall, behind Peter, were taped pictures and stories of traffic accidents clipped from newspapers and magazines.

Dom was huge. Never in his life had Ian seen anyone as large, and he forced himself to concentrate on the curtain, imagining what was behind it so that he would not stare. Dom's body was whacked out of proportion, ill-sized and mismatched; his hands were delicate, his face petite, almost pretty, but the rest of his body was bloated and ringed with fat. His joints, elbows and wrists were hairline creases in full rolls of skin, and the skin itself was as dull and greasy as cold wax. He sat pinched into a small low swivel chair with his huge doughy buttocks sloughed over the seat. A broad plastic mat was set on the floor so that he could shunt himself from the desk to the sink without having to rise from his chair; every slight move solicited a sigh. The next and greater shock was Dom's voice, which, each time he heard it, rose the hairs on his arms. Soft, alluring, and distinctly feminine, it poured out of the man and thickened in the room, seductive and nocturnal. This was not the man that Ian had spoken with from his sister's.

Space was so limited that when Dom moved, so, it seemed, must everyone else, accommodating a body that had to, Ian thought, easily occupy one-sixth of the room. Mentally dividing the room, he quantified Dom against the other occupants. The man was wider than his desk. One cyclist sat beside the desk reading a newspaper, and every time Dom reached past him – as he was in the way of the counter, the kettle, and the sink – the rider braced himself back without bothering to lower his paper. Ferret-like, long and wiry, his face was narrow, with small copper-brown eyes, and short light-brown hair. Lithe and alert, he was the exact opposite of Dom. He smiled at the paper as he read, and Ian felt that he was being watched, assessed, and several times he caught the man looking at his right arm and splint. Affecting disinterest, Ian stared indifferently back, reading the words 'Yeah, Yeah, Noh' printed in faint grey letters across a T-shirt that might once have been white.

Four other riders waited, either reading or drinking coffee. All but one, Ian thought, were about his age. Settled beside and under their seats were wide-mouthed shoulder bags. Most of the riders wore T-shirts, sweaters, cycling shorts or frayed cut-off jeans, showing broad sturdy knees and muscular legs. Across the various shins and forearms were the bluish stamps of tattoos and the purple shadows of healed scabs.

Dom asked for Ian's name a second time. Daintily cocking an eyebrow he rose his voice and asked Peter if he thought that his friend was ready. Peter nodded without turning from his magazine, and Dom sat back, smiling as if his question were funny. It was hard for Ian to look at Dom without thinking that this was, without doubt, the fattest man he'd ever seen. But foremost he was conscious of his arm, and he waited for Dom's questions, but they did not come. As Dom explained how the calls worked, the rider with the 'Yeah, Yeah, Noh' T-shirt lowered his paper and watched.

Ian's first job was to collect a package from an advertising agency on Fleet Street and deliver it to the Associated Press Offices less than three streets away. W1 to W1. £3. The agency also sold rubber shoulder bags, which Ian was told he needed as most of the packages would be too broad for his panniers. It could not sound, Ian thought, any easier.

The man with the 'Yeah, Yeah, Noh' T-shirt came up the stairs after him, and for a moment they both stood squinting in the sunlight, blinking. The man's bike was small, as compact as a toy, and secured to a bollard with a thick steel chain. He unfastened his lock and slung the chain over his shoulders in one smooth gesture, then straddled his bike, ready to go, while Ian still fumbled with his lock.

The man was wearing army boots and no socks, his legs were shaved, and the muscles along his thighs and calves were taut and compact. He watched Ian wrestle with the radio holster, and reaching forward he untwisted the strap around Ian's neck.

'You've not done this before then?'

'Two days once.' Ian shook his head, recognizing the man's voice from the telephone.

'How do you think you'll manage?'

Ian shrugged. The man looked at the handlebars. On the right-hand side the brake lever was mounted under the rubber grip and wrapped with gaffer-tape so that his fingers could grip more easily. The man nodded, satisfied.

'Derek,' he offered his left hand.

Ian tightened the straps around his wrist as Derek explained with some patience the same information that Dom had hurried through – how to check the batteries, what channel to keep the radio on, and how to respond when Dom called. The system was simple, there were twelve riders, each with their own call number: Derek was 04, Peter was 07, and Ian was 09. The worst thing you could do was to respond to someone else's call. This was all that Ian needed to remember, everything else he could muddle through.

'One battery should last you the day. Don't recharge unless it's fully spent.' He showed Ian the serial number stamped on a foil strip on the battery's heel so that he could remember which of the batteries still held a full charge. Some, he said, were better than others.

They were ready to leave when Peter came up and on to the street. Peter looked quickly at Derek without smiling, then reattached the front wheel to his bike without a word to either of them.

Derek rode close to Ian, keeping to his right-hand side. When Ian reached the first set of traffic lights Derek was no longer beside him, and he couldn't see him back down the street. After he crossed the junction Derek returned on his left-hand side, a small carton of orange juice in his hand. He offered the carton to Ian, who refused, knowing he'd drop it, but Derek insisted.

'Take the whole thing,' he said. 'Take it for later.'

Ian turned to see Peter barrelling down upon them. With cars parked on either side the street seemed too narrow for him to pass, but with one swift curve he swooped around and hurtled on as smooth and direct as if he had cycled through them.

Derek looked after him, nodding. 'He's good,' he said, 'very good', with neither admiration nor envy.

The lobby at the Hunter & Nicholson Agency was an immense steel-trimmed hall with a glass roof, chrome-railed balconies, and sleek vertiginous black marble columns. A porter in a black cap and dress-coat stood guard beside the desk, his hands clasped behind him and his chest thrust out pigeon-like. Ex-army, Ian thought. Short and stocky, the man reminded him of Gordon's father.

The porter signalled Ian forward to the desk. Ian repeated Dom's instructions and the man reached over the counter and immediately handed him the package. A copy of the *Daily Mirror* was open on the counter. Beneath a picture of Sumpter was a smaller photograph of his mother. The man was paralyzed, the caption said, and unable to talk.

'Both go to the AP.' The porter offered Ian a second package, saying that he hadn't called the pick-up in.

Ian took the package, recognizing that this was some kind of a favour. On top of the package were four pound coins, and he understood that if he didn't tell Western about the job, he could keep the money.

Ian remembered that he needed a delivery bag. This was, he guessed, probably the first job that Dom gave his new couriers. The clerk pointed over his shoulder telling him to go all the way back to dispatch.

The distribution office was shabbily chaotic, and the woman assisting him handed him the bag and refused payment, waving her hand and telling him to 'take it. I wouldn't know where to put the money if you paid me anyway.' She called him love. A nice word, he thought, to hear from a stranger.

Outside, he unlocked his bike, tucked the packages safely in his bag, then adjusted the straps around his wrist. His palms were sweating, and catching his full reflection in the office window he was surprised and pleased to see that he looked like any other messenger.

At three thirty Ian climbed the back stairs to the third floor of a warehouse behind Soho Mews, heading to the offices of a company called On-Line Productions. In his bag was another pick-up, airline tickets from a travel agent at Oxford Circus for a lawyer at Temple Bar. His calves, knees, thighs, and lower back were aching and tight. Through the window he could see the Post Office Tower. On every floor were small graphic or advertising companies; it was his third visit in two hours, and he was irritated with running back and forth to the same building. Most of the creative businesses had dull, pedantic names – Tru-Colour Photo, Speedy Design, Vector Graphics – and their stairwells and lobbies were hung with framed certificates embossed with the words Best, National, or British.

The secretary at On-Line sat under a wall of awards with the phone snucked between her jaw and shoulder. She flipped indolently through a diary, unable to fix an appointment. The office smelled of the rich, welcoming scents of ground coffee and linseed oil. On a desk made of one single curve of wood was a flat brown envelope, there was little else in the office.

Up and running all day, Ian was now tired. Hurrying in and out of offices, surrounded by people in taxis, cars, buses, and avoiding pedestrians was more exhausting than he expected. The pauses, stops and waits were unwelcome interruptions at first, but now after a whole day of cycling, the breaks seemed less frequent.

'She's out of town,' the secretary flipped forward a page. 'I'll see if she's back before then.' The woman rolled her eyes.

Without warning Ian's radio crackled out loud, 'Hank-the-Wank, Hank-the-Wank. That's w-a-n-k. Hank-the-Wank. Pick-up for 07 at Lincoln's Inn Fields.' Dom's voice sputtered and sang into the office, well aware of the trouble he might cause. Without looking up the secretary narrowed her eyes. Pointing at the package she told Ian that he was being paid to deliver the package, not stare at it. What was he waiting for? Picking up the envelope, she held it out, mouthing that he should be very, very careful, as if she were talking to an imbecile. Did he understand?

Ian reached for the envelope but the woman would not let go. She stared at his right arm, then speaking into the telephone, asked if the person could wait.

'What happened to the other messenger?'

Ian shrugged.

'The one with the accent. The South African. We usually have someone else.'

'He's in hospital. Traction.' Ian tapped his heels together to verify the lie.

The secretary looked down at her desk.

'I can't give this to you.'

Holding firmly onto the envelope Ian asked why not.

The woman looked quickly at his arm and then back at the envelope.

Ian told her that she could call another company if she wasn't comfortable with the service. When she didn't reply he lightly tugged the packet from her hand and slipped it into his shoulder bag.

The radio burped as he headed for the door, and he heard her complain, exasperation growing in her voice, 'last week one of them fell down the stairs, and this week we have one with a broken arm.'

Stamping down the stairs two at a time, Ian fought hard with the compunction to fold the envelope in half. Who was this moron who couldn't tell the difference between an Irish and a South African accent?

Finding a spent matchstick on the mat inside the door, he

broke it in half then jammed it into the buzzer. He walked away calmer to a faint and irritated, 'Hello – hello – hello?'

Ian's last job was a delivery to Temple Bar. Essex Court. It amazed him to discover a whole network of buildings huddled between Fleet Street and the Thames, folding endlessly and protectively in on themselves. Connected through tight passageways that opened into one paved courtyard after another, their brick backs turned to the outside world, much like a convent, he thought, or a boarding school. The barristers' names were painted on long white boards mounted on either side of the doorways, even so, it took him a while to find the office he wanted.

Inside, the hallways were tiny and narrow with soft, cool plaster walls slightly out of perpendicular. The doors were petite, the floors a dark malty polished wood. Ian breathed deeply, enjoying the fusty luxury. The secretary smiled as he walked into the office. Adjusting a bright red headband she drew her hair back, several clips in her mouth, and said that she was waiting for him. It was the end of the day for them both, and she looked organised, untroubled, her desk cleared of business. Ian felt grubby and worn. The woman accepted the envelope with a pleasant smile.

'Shouldn't I sign something? I usually do.'

Ian shook his head.

'Why don't you sit down for five minutes?'

Ian hesitated and the woman smiled broadly. 'Go on. You look like you've been busy.'

Ian did as he was told, surprised that the woman was talking to him. Once he sat down he didn't know what to do.

The secretary looked quickly at the tickets and set them in a drawer. Beside her desk was an empty fireplace, and above it hung a small lacquered painting of a racehorse. Thoroughbred, Ian thought. The office had the refined air of a gentleman's club.

The woman logged off her computer, and as she waited for the screen to close she asked after Dom. How was he doing?

Ian explained that this was his first day, and she looked at him, thinking, before she switched off the computer. 'He was in hospital for a month. We did some business for him when he first moved to Endell Street.' Her voice was full of affection. 'Tell him I said hello.'

Ian's forearm itched under the support, and he tried to scratch, not wanting to take the splint off in the office. The secretary asked if he wanted a letter opener, saying that she remembered how her arm itched after she broke hers. Ian said thanks but no thanks.

'How did you do it?'

'Riding accident.'

'Bicycle?'

'No.'

'You ride horses?' There was surprise in her voice.

Ian shook his head. 'Kicked by a donkey on Blackpool sands.'

'Now why do I know that isn't true?' Lifting a small leather shoulder-bag on to the table the secretary told him that he was going to get on well with Dom.

Leaving the office, it occurred to Ian just how much he liked the job. He liked being able to walk into the middle of other people's working lives, and it amazed him that except for two comments, everyone would trust packages and documents to a bicycle messenger with one fully-functional arm. Tomorrow, he thought, if anyone gave him any trouble he would pretend to be partially deaf.

Locked in the middle of the courtyard was Peter's bike. Ian walked up and down looking into the basement offices, enjoying the shade and chill thrown off the cold brick buildings, but he could not find him.

Dom rummaged through his desk as Ian returned his radio.

Ian waited for some nasty comment but it didn't come. He knew that he was late and thought that he was keeping Dom at work. Dom held his hand out for Ian's dockets and asked how many runs he'd done, saying it probably wasn't as easy as he thought. He reminded Ian to keep a separate tally of his jobs, as his accounting, he chuckled, was sometimes a little creative. Ian couldn't be sure if Dom was joking.

Removing the battery from the radio he pushed it into the charger. There were several other stacks of dockets on the desk, all dog-eared, and all thicker than his. The red light blinked on the battery pack, and Dom watched, his mind comfortably settled elsewhere.

Ian said goodbye and took the stairs two at a time. The day was done, he was tired, his legs were sore and his backside numb from the hard plastic bicycle seat. The splint was chafing his arm, a bath would soon soothe it and he doubted that he would have any trouble sleeping.

Back on the street, Peter sat in the shade, smoking and resting against the open door. Avoiding Peter's shadow, Ian stepped into the street. Peter smiled as he unlocked his bike. They agreed that it was an unusually warm day for March.

'Which way do you go?'

Ian pointed towards Covent Garden, thinking for a moment that he did not want to return to Gordon's.

'And you?'

Peter pointed towards High Holborn. He held up his pouch of tobacco. Inside were several rolled cigarettes, neatly pinched at one end. Removing his splint Ian took one, then sat beside Peter, and spent the next five minutes in silence, smoking and massaging his arm, enjoying the quiet and the sun on his face. Peter looked out at the street through half-closed eyes, his wrists resting on his knees. In one hand was a slip of paper, a prediction from the tourist shop in Leicester Square. The paper was blank except for an embossed border, dark in one corner where Peter had rubbed the raised pattern. The other predictions suggested that some sense could be made from their garbled sentences, but this one didn't have anything to say. As Ian looked, Peter leaned closer to him, and running his finger along the border their arms brushed. He said that this would be his last fortune, he'd spent enough money, and Ian agreed. It seemed like a good place to stop.

Peter continued talking. Ian listened, but did not pay attention, lost instead in the supple cadence of Peter's voice. He found himself agreeing that he also wanted to bike through France, and he remembered his agreement to return to Amsterdam with Gordon.

Once again, Gordon was not home. There were three messages on the answering machine. One from Terry asking after his brother, and two from Gordon. The first asking if Ian could feed Buster, and the other to say that he talked with Louise this morning, and she was thinking of moving out of London and back to her parents. Had she talked with Ian about this? He would, he said, be back from Leicester tomorrow.

'By the way,' he said. 'I called you at work today and some joker said you'd quit?'

Ian erased the messages, then searched through the house for the cat. Finding her curled on the couch with the sun on her back he picked her up. Holding her close he talked to her with a mock Irish accent, saying that he thought that Gordon was in Kettering and not Leicester.

At ten o'clock Ian was woken by the telephone. The ring sounded unusually loud and he hurried to the phone telling himself that if he let the answering machine pick up it would be Gordon, but if he picked up before the machine it would certainly be someone else. The street outside was silent. To his surprise the voice was Dom's, and for a moment he thought that he was being fired, and that Dom was calling to tell him not to come in tomorrow.

'We need toilet paper. Bring it in tomorrow would you? White, soft, unscented. I'll reimburse you on Friday and bring me a newspaper and milk.'

Dom's voice weltered out of the machine and sweetened the room. Picking up the phone Ian asked what kind of milk Dom wanted. Dom answered quickly that any kind of milk from a cow would do.

Across London, Ian thought, from the city to the suburbs, there must be people hopelessly smitten by Dom's voice. As he slunk back into bed with a hot-water bottle crooked under his arm, Ian wondered at the kind of a body they fleshed his voice out with.

He looked at the clock. It was ten past ten, and his new boss was calling him for toilet paper.

After buying Dom's supplies and three newspapers Ian cycled hard down Walworth Road to the Elephant and Castle. Arriving at Waterloo Bridge he realized that he was not concentrating. Conscious that he should be more careful, he began to make mistakes. Trying to cut through a set of traffic lights, he blocked pedestrians at a crossing. One man bellowed at him, indignantly stamping his feet. 'Why don't you run me over?' The lights changed, and as Ian wheeled off he told the man that he was much too fat to be run over by a bicycle. Barely through the junction and into Aldwych, he thought of Dom and regretted the insult.

The office was as dark as the day before, and just as airless. Dom sat at his desk with his chin slumped deep into his neck and his mouth set in a sulk. Ian gave Dom the toilet rolls and two newspapers, wondering for a moment which he would prefer. A new courier, Rhino, sat at the foot of the stairs blocking the way. Much younger than the other riders and more talkative, Rhino's head was shaved except for a small starched-white tuft centred high on his forehead. Dom leafed through the newspapers imperiously clucking his tongue, tolerating the boy's chatter before telling him, curtly, to either shut up or take it outside. The boy sat back and sulkily folded his arms, but before long, began to chatter again, asking Ian what was wrong with his arm. Ian replied quickly and vaguely that it was the consequence of talking to the wrong person at the wrong time. Dom smiled at his newspaper, then asked a second time if they both wouldn't mind shutting up. A gauzy blue hood of smoke hung a foot below the ceiling.

By nine o'clock everyone except Derek and Peter had arrived, and the riders waited for the calls to start. Dom shuffled papers around his desk and said several times that it was going to be a slow day.

Peter arrived at ten past nine, completing one delivery from the previous day; he set his satchel on the seat beside Ian with a quiet hello. In the fluorescent light his upper arms appeared thin and white, the skinny arms, Ian thought, of a boy who spent his summers indoors, not the arms of an athlete or a cyclist. There was a pocket of shadow under Peter's eyes and he looked sleepy, barely awake. His hair was wet and combed straight back, and as he bent forward searching through his satchel Ian could smell a sweet apple-like scent of shampoo. Peter's vest was slightly open and Ian idly wondered how soft Peter's skin would be. As he sat down, still searching through his bag, he zipped up his vest, but the thought stuck in Ian's mind.

Peter emptied his pack of groceries, handing several packets of instant soup, two rolls of Digestive biscuits, some cream crackers, and a pack of Benson & Hedges to Dom. Thanking him, Dom cleared his throat and said that it was going to be quiet today. 'I doubt you'll get your fifty.'

Peter sat back and folded his arms, the only person to have understood Dom's comment.

By three fifteen Ian was almost up to Hampstead. There was

a slight head wind, barely enough to disturb the leaves on the trees but enough to feel a constant resistance. He called Gordon twice, leaving a message both times on his mobile and at home; wherever he was he would be able to retrieve his messages. Ian doubted that he would make anything on the Hampstead pick-up; the longer it took the more jobs he would lose in the city, but the day was passing quickly and he was happy to be occupied. That morning he was paid to wake someone up on Whitfield Street. Money in pocket. £4 for an eleven o'clock wake-up call.

With less than two hours left Peter had completed thirty-seven jobs, and listening to Peter's dispatch calls Ian understood that he was hoping to complete fifty pick-ups in the one day. There was some excitement among the other messengers, and for most of his ride to Bath Road Ian was accompanied by a running commentary of Peter sightings. Everyone except Rhino was keeping count of Peter's jobs.

The addresses on Bath Road stopped at 70, and the further Ian cycled the less certain he was that he was on the right track. There was no number 76. Having confirmed the number with Dom, Ian was reluctant to ask again, and it was a relief when Dom called, saying that the client was pestering him. Where was he? What could possibly take him so long? Was he walking? Ian wrestled the radio free from its holster and relayed his location. Bath Road. NW3.

Dom called back, confused, did Ian say North West Three, and not West One?

There was an awful silence while they both realized Ian's mistake.

'09 come back in and give me a call when you reach Regent's Park. I have a new pick-up at Regent's Park.' There was a tone of resignation rather than irritation in Dom's voice. Heedless of the traffic, Ian turned the bike around and headed back, cycling hard, angry at his mistake and embarrassed that everyone would have heard it.

'I have a job at Bath Road, West One. West, repeat, West One. Is there anyone remotely close?'

Peter responded immediately. He was close, he could take the job.

'Negative, 07,' Dom replied, 'you have a pick-up at Gower Street, Hank-the-Wank at three-thirty, then I have another set to take you over your mark.'

'I'm at the door,' Peter said. 'If it's Trevor Stuart, I'm at the door. I can deliver before Lincoln's Inn. Give 09 the Gower Street.'

'Go ahead.' Now Dom sounded irritated, and Ian wished that Peter hadn't taken the job.

Dom immediately called Ian back asking if he was at Regent's Park yet? 'I have a pick-up at Cumberland Terrace. Fourteen – one, four – Cumberland Terrace. Private residence. After that there's a pick-up on Gower Street, University Hospital. Confirm the Cumberland pick-up and I'll give you the particulars.'

Ian wrote the details on separate dockets. The radio sputtered and he paused, listening, as Dom congratulated Peter, 'I have your total at forty. Don't deliver your Bath Road, go directly to Hank-the-Wank.'

Several of the riders whooped and hollered over the radio, their thin voices loud enough to turn drivers' heads as Ian set off.

Dom gave Ian another two jobs when he called in from Cumberland Terrace. Ian stopped to plot his route drawing on the A-Z, organizing the pick-ups and drop-offs in his head. This meant money, good money, and if he didn't get rattled, he thought, he could manage. He checked the map several times, closed the book, opened it and checked again. As he set off it began to rain; small gobbets, not even drizzle. Cars seized up the smaller streets, and Ian guessed that the poor weather would mean more work, and more money.

Less than two minutes later Peter called through and said that he was being tested. Dom asked him to repeat his message.

'Arrested,' Peter said. 'The police. I'm being arrested. Can someone come and get my bike. I'm at Bath Road and the Strand. I haven't made the pick-up.' Dom quickly reassured Peter and asked for the closest rider. Rhino answered the call saying that he was already on the Strand, he had to see this.

Four fifteen and heading into the West End, Ian waited at the lights in heavy rain on Shaftesbury Avenue and High Holborn. The road was slick and water scattered off the backs of the buses; he was miserable. There was no news of Peter; whatever happened had happened while he was picking up Ian's job.

Everything Ian was wearing was wet, not just wet, but saturated, dense and heavy; only the radio wrapped in a plastic shopping bag and the inside of his satchel were dry. The pages of his A-Z were sodden and difficult to read. Coming up in the other direction and stopped at the lights was another messenger. Derek. They recognized each other and Derek shouted and laughed and held his long arms out and his face up to the rain. His shirt stuck to his body. There was nothing to do but give in to it.

The lights changed, but before any traffic crossed the junction a cyclist sped through. Ian immediately recognized Peter, hunched down to the handlebars, thin white arms and shoulders, his head tilted, shifting his weight to swerve his bike surely between the two lanes of traffic. Then he was swiftly gone. Derek and Ian both hooted and clapped and shook their fists in the air. Derek called in on the radio.

'04, 07 sighted at High Holborn. Free at last. Free at last. What job is this?'

'04,' Dom replied, '07 is on job forty-four. 07 call me for a three-job package running from Cavendish Square to Aldwych, call me at your Wigmore drop-off. All riders, I have four thirty runs to Paddington and New Oxford Street. Open call, first to respond.'

Ian was standing in a doorway on Farringdon Road watching the rain when Dom called Peter for the forty-eighth pick-up. WC2 to WC2. Adams Street to Langley Lane. His voice sounded hard, disappointed, and he apologized for such a small job, saying that it was the last pick-up of the day. Peter replied with a modest thank-you. Several other riders called to congratulate him. Ian recognized Derek's voice and was too embarrassed to call. If Peter hadn't been arrested he would have made his fifty jobs.

Away over Islington the clouds broke to a wide, cold, opal blue, but above him, leaning all the way west, the sky remained a solid battleship grey.

By the time Ian returned to Endell Street the sun was out again and his clothes were almost dry. He was even later than he was on his first day.

Derek sat in Dom's chair rolling himself a cigarette with his feet up and his boots set on Dom's table, and his biking clothes in a bag slumped on the counter. Dom stood with one hand steadying himself against the counter, the other punching buttons on the microwave.

Turning his chair around, Derek said hi, and held a cigarette up to his mouth, licking along its length to seal it. His shirt was unbuttoned, and through his left nipple was a small silver ring, just large enough to crown his little finger. He looked satisfied, happy that the day was over, and he stretched out in the chair, arching his back to reach into his pocket for his lighter.

'Wet enough?'

Ian told him that the sun was back out.

'How many did you manage today?' he asked, smiling up, the first blue flush of smoke clouding his mouth then softly dispersing. Ian couldn't look at him without noticing the nipple ring.

'Twenty. If the wait-and-returns count as two.'

Dom shook his head. 'Wait-and-returns are one job,' he said tartly, turning slowly to face the room. The microwave hummed behind him.

'But it's £1 per minute waiting, which is your money.' Derek looked at the dockets in Ian's hands. The papers were sodden from the rain. 'You marked down the waiting time?'

Ian slowly shook his head. Of course he hadn't. He'd done even less work than the previous day.

Trailing one hand on the counter, Dom toddled to his desk with short shuffling steps. Derek scooted the chair out of his way, and Dom paused, leaning hard against his desk. It wasn't more than four or five short steps from the microwave to the desk, but the walk clearly required an effort. Finding a pen and some coins Dom asked Ian for his dockets.

'Always make sure you charge for waiting.' He pushed the money across the desk top, and Ian noticed that his fingernails were neatly manicured, the quicks pushed evenly back. Dom asked if Ian would run and get some cigarettes. Benson & Hedges. Ian remembered seeing two fresh packets that morning. How could he have smoked them all?

Derek asked if the radio battery was flat. Ian said no, and Derek told him to keep the radio until tomorrow. 'Run it down,' he said. 'Otherwise the batteries are no good after a while.'

Ian asked what happened with Peter and the police. Dom waved his hand over his shoulder, clearly irritated. 'Someone called for you earlier. He wouldn't leave a name or a message.'

Puzzled, Ian asked what the man looked like. Dom turned to Derek and shrugged. 'He was here an hour ago.'

'Did he have a goatee?'

Dom nodded, and Ian did not doubt that it was Gordon. He must, he thought, be back from Leicester.

Pausing at the bottom of the stairs, he carefully rolled up his right sleeve and took off his splint to inspect his forearm. What, he wondered, did Gordon want? Watching him, Derek asked what was wrong with his arm, and Ian replied that it was a long story, it would take a whole evening to tell and a number of beers. Derek smiled, his hand over his chest, absently teasing the nipple ring. He said fair enough, maybe later in the week then? Dom asked impatiently for his cigarettes. If he didn't mind, he said, it would be nice to get them today.

Peter was sitting in the doorway when Ian returned with the cigarettes. His hair dried flat to his forehead, he looked tired and irritated and did not notice Ian until he was standing directly over him. Ian told him that he was sorry about the police, he felt responsible.

Peter looked up as if the thought hadn't occurred to him. 'They were just messing with me,' he shrugged, dismissing the incident. 'It's happened before.'

Ian stepped by Peter saying that he was keeping Dom waiting. He held up the pack of cigarettes to explain himself. Before Ian was down the stairs Peter asked if he was interested in a beer perhaps. Ian said yes, then immediately regretted his answer, wanting instead to return home to see Gordon.

Back in his chair, Dom asked if that was Peter upstairs. 'Tomorrow,' he said, 'I'll keep you local. Soho and the Courts.'

Keeping him on shorter runs, he thought, might be some kind of probation, he could not tell. Derek sat in one of the fold-up chairs, elbow on the counter. He asked Ian what he was doing and Ian told him that he was going for a drink with Peter. Dom said there were beers in the fridge that Ian was welcome to. They'd been there for a long time and should be drunk.

Ian handed the cigarettes to Dom, then took the last two beers from the fridge, holding the bottles by their wet necks. Dom picked the cellophane off the packet, breathing heavily through his mouth, and Ian guessed that he shouldn't be smoking. As he returned back up the stairs he felt a sudden wave of sympathy and asked if there was anything that Dom wanted him to bring tomorrow.

Dom waved his hand over his shoulder, telling him to take the beers and sod off home.

Ian handed one of the beers to Peter explaining that they were from Dom. Peter waited for Ian to sit beside him before he twisted the cap off, and said that it was nice, this, being here. On his left wrist was a bulky black watch. Ian asked if it was new. Peter covered the watch with his hand. It was a gift from his sister. It was his birthday. She gave it to him that morning but he only put it on in the afternoon while he was in the police car. It took almost an hour to calibrate.

Taking the watch off, he handed it to Ian and explained with growing animation how it worked. Still measuring Peter's heart-rate, the numbers flickered and changed with a slight stutter. Peter unzipped his vest to show the other half of the gadget, a black rubberized strap banded around his chest. A red crease ran an inch under his nipples where the band pinched into his skin. Ian held the watch up to Peter's chest and watched his skin pulse softly; the numbers fluttered and changed in perfect time. Peter said that there were another two parts to it on the hub and fork of his front wheel, which told the watch his speed and distance. 'I've cycled 9.37 miles since my four-thirty pick-up from Hank-the-Wank.'

Ian asked who Hank-the-Wank was, and Peter laughed. Hank-the-Wank was a lawyer at Lincoln's Inn Fields. William Hanker called the same time every day and asked specifically for Peter. Ian still did not understand the name and Peter explained that the man sat with his chair shoved tight to his desk, with one hand stuffed in his pocket. Peter kneaded his crotch and they both winced. Peter shrugged, laughing. 'There's worse. Much worse.'

Ian asked about Dom and Western and Peter said that there wasn't much to tell, except that Dom and Derek started the company together a long time ago. They'd been together a long, long time, eleven, twelve years, he wasn't sure. Ian asked if Dom lived in the office. It was a joke of sorts, but Peter nodded, as far as he knew Dom lived in the cellar. It hardly seemed possible. Lowering his voice, Ian quizzed him: where was the bed, his clothes, how could he wash? and Peter answered that there was a curtain under the stairs, and behind it another room with a mattress, a toilet, and a shower.

It was strange, almost inconceivable to Ian that a man who spent his life in a cellar would have such an intimate knowledge of the city, and that it would be his business to send people about it. He carelessly said that it was sad, and Peter disagreed. In two years he hadn't seen Dom anywhere other than the basement of Endell Street, but it didn't mean that he didn't or couldn't get out, or that he was unhappy.

'Derek looks after him,' he said, 'and Dom isn't shy about asking for anything he needs.'

'What about his family?'

'He has Derek, and his books. His room is full of books.'

Ian asked Peter what he meant and Peter paused and suddenly flushed, and glanced quickly back into the dark stairwell. Sitting up, he asked Ian what the time was. The only thing his watch didn't do was tell the time, he said. He was meeting his sister at the Festival Hall, there was a film if Ian was interested, but he couldn't remember what it was.

'It's something that Jennah bought tickets for.'

Ian said that he should return to Gordon's, but would go with him as far as the South Bank.

Ian followed Peter to the Seven Dials, thinking that he should call Gordon. Peter waited at the corner, then stepped back on his bike and was off as soon as Ian caught up. Ian had barely started pedalling when Peter was already at the next junction.

He cut down Bedford to Garrick and across the Strand, moving swiftly and without hesitation, slipping through the late rush-hour traffic, it looked easy, effortless, and beautiful; intimidated by the traffic Ian was considerably slower.

They walked their bikes over Hungerford Bridge. A breeze cut down the river, and there it all was, Westminster to the City, laid out in a wide arc – Parliament, the Abbey, Whitehall, Charing Cross, Somerset House, and a distant St Paul's – London's brave face, tempered by fires, plagues, and the Blitz. Look in the other direction, Ian thought, and you're staring up its nubby arse.

Ian asked if Peter liked London. Peter squinted back at the city, not caring particularly one way or another. He shrugged and grinned and said that today wasn't the best day to answer, but yes, why not, he liked the place enough. Peter asked Ian where he lived.

It wasn't an easy question to answer. Ian explained that he moved to London about nine months ago. 'I stayed with a friend, Gordon, for the first couple of weeks, then found a place through a squatter's co-op on Railton Road. We were evicted last week. Police, dogs, the whole works.' He started to explain about the squat, and as he spoke he realized that everything needed to be qualified with a further explanation. He knew Gordon from home, and he knew Malc through Gordon, as Gordon was working with Malc's brother. He met Louise at the squatter's co-op. It was unnecessarily complicated, and hearing himself talk he wondered why anyone would be sympathetic. It was only Louise's tenuous agreement with the council that made Hopewell seem so secure, an agreement which the council could renege on at any time. If you squatted a house, you expected to be evicted. It wasn't so unreasonable or even much of a surprise. Peter disagreed. They were evicted for someone else's profit, why else would the council bother? These days everyone with money wanted a small terraced house with a garden close to the tube, and the councils couldn't sell the places fast enough.

'If I knew it would be this much trouble I wouldn't have done it.' Ian looked along the South Bank, at the concrete bunkers of theatres and exhibition halls. Everything was built as close as possible to the river, marooned by default on the south side. Even the supports for the London Eye struck into the Thames, half-on half-off the Embankment. 'I've known Gordon for a long time, and when he moved to London I assumed at some point that I would too.'

'How long have you known him?'

'Eighteen, nineteen years?'

'See that building.' Peter stopped and pointed up the river. He drew Ian close so that he could see the short brick tower pointing above the white stone of Waterloo Bridge. One step in either direction and the tower disappeared behind the black glassy walls of city offices. 'It's a prep school. Chapel Bar. Dom used to teach there.'

Peter leaned against the rail, and spreading his arms he stroked his hands over the wooden runner and looked out over the Thames. There was a barge at the end of Festival Pier and a party was beginning to disembark. One man gathered in the pennants. The tide was turning, showing the dark, rotten legs of the pier and the inky stained river walls. The pontoon ducked as the barge tugged away from it. Peter folded his arms and looked back up the river.

'They're a couple. Dom and Derek. A couple.'

Ian leaned uncertainly forward. Peter nodded and continued talking, making it obvious that he was not joking. 'They've been together for a very long time. Derek was working for another messenger service when they met. It was his idea to start Western.'

Ian left Peter at Waterloo Bridge, and Peter lingered for a

moment before returning back to meet his sister at the Festival Hall.

The ride home was easy, eventless; Ian was surprised by the news about Derek and Dom. The notion that the two men, so physically different, were a couple seemed implausible, unless, of course, the attachment was sentimental. That Dom could be queer, or even sexual, posed no problem for him, but he couldn't picture the two men together. The longer he considered it, the less sense the relationship made.

The traffic was slow on the Walworth Road and he wove dozily between the taxis and buses. As he waited at the traffic lights he wiped his face, he could smell exhaust on his hand. Some people in the street were wearing sweaters and anoraks, others T-shirts, confused by the changeable weather.

As soon as he opened the front door Ian could smell bacon frying. Gordon was home. Ian called up the stairs, shouting above the noise of the radio, and Gordon came out to the landing with a fork in his hand. Leaning against the banisters, he watched as Ian lumbered his bike up the stairs.

Gordon pointed at the bike and asked Ian what was going on. Ian stopped, the bicycle becoming suddenly awkward and cumbersome, as he explained that he was working as a messenger. 'I started yesterday. Did you come round to the office earlier?'

Gordon walked back into the kitchen without answering.

Leaning his bike against the banisters Ian followed after him, asking a second time if Gordon came down to Western Messengers at around three or four o'clock?

Turning off the stove Gordon set the hot frying pan on the kitchen table. He said that he knew nothing about the job, so he wouldn't know where the office was then, would he?

'Then who came to the office?'

'I don't know.'

'Did you get my messages?'

Gordon nodded and looked at his watch. He was waiting for a call, he said.

Everything was set to the right side of the table. Unsettled, Ian moved the ketchup and used cups to the left side. Gordon told him to leave everything as it was.

'Why do you always have to do that?'

Ian asked about his trip to Kettering, and Gordon shrugged, clearly irritated. Since the burglary everything was unsettled, the occupants fled without paying rent and the police were pestering him about every property that Patterson owned in Kettering and Leicester. Gordon was uncomfortable with the disorder. It would be ugly if they started asking about London, not everything that Patterson was doing was above board. It was nothing short of a complete fuck-up and he regretted keeping the job after Terry quit. Gordon helped himself to two slices of bread.

'I thought you were in Kettering?'

'I was.'

'Your call last night was from Leicester.'

Gordon picked up the bacon and let the grease drip slowly back into the pan. 'I was in Leicester when I called. What of it?'

Ian asked if he had heard anything more from Louise.

'Not since Sunday.' Tearing his sandwich in two Gordon gave half to Ian and asked him what he thought he was doing cycling in London. What was he trying to prove?

Ian dipped the sandwich into the grease and waited, counting, watching the fat soak into the bread.

'Who put this idea into your head?' Gordon pointed at his arm. 'You didn't come up with this. What about your other job?'

Ian replied bluntly that he quit because it was a stupid job, and they were probably going to fire him anyway.

Gordon finished his half of the sandwich and said with his

mouth half-full that what was stupid was working on the bikes. There was no other word for it.

Ian shrugged and said that he must be stupid then, but it was a good job with good people, and besides he was careful and what else was he supposed to do?

Dissatisfied, Gordon said that Ian should go back to his old job. 'I'll pay you. I'm serious. I'll pay you. I'll give you good money.'

The telephone rang and Gordon strode into the hall. Standing over the phone he waited for the answering machine. Ian recognized Terry's voice, but Gordon did not pick up. Ian wiped the pan clean with another slice of bread and stared out at the garden as he ate, suddenly fed up. His job was none of Gordon's business. The cat sat at the door with her back turned to him.

After Terry hung up, Gordon sat on the stairs to make a call. He spoke in a soft voice, his back to the banisters and shoulders turned away from the kitchen. On the kitchen table Gordon's mobile rang, and Terry N. appeared on the display. Beside the phone was Patterson's ledger. Beside the ledger was Gordon's passport.

Gordon returned to the kitchen, picked up his mobile and deleted the message without reading it. Was Ian still hungry? If he fancied they could go to Sharma's. He'd buy, but first he had to make a run over to Deptford. Patterson was pestering him for the rents. Ian recognized the offer as a bribe.

'How about it?' he asked, looking out at the garden. 'Did you think about what I said?'

Ian said that there was nothing to think about, he was keeping the job, there was no question of returning to the Department of Employment. 'I'm happy doing this. I like the people I work with.' There was much more to say, but Gordon would not listen.

As they drove to Deptford Gordon pointed at the businesses

that he collected rents from – mini-marts, newsagents, and launderettes, living rooms turned into off-licences and cut-price clothing stores – telling stories of people who could or could not be trusted, as if the money they owed were his own. In every instance the apartments above the shops were vacant, or used, as far as Ian could tell, as storage. Tucked beside Gordon's seat was Patterson's slim black zippered wallet, along with the post from the burgled house. Among the letters were two familiar brown envelopes, benefit cheques.

Patterson allowed Gordon to use one of his cars for three days each month to collect the rents. The Jaguar – second-hand and refitted – was Patterson's one indulgence. Gordon also used the car for errands, driving to Peckham or Lewisham to buy milk or cigarettes, although there were shops within easy walking distance of his house. Nine months before, Gordon had met Ian at Victoria Station with the same car, and every time he sat in it Ian remembered their smooth untroubled run through London, and how impressed he was on that first day by the unsubtle luxury of soft beige leather, the cigar-like smell, and his friend's apparent success.

Ian called Louise on Gordon's mobile, but the line was dead. As he redialled the number the mobile started to ring and he passed it to Gordon.

Checking the caller ID, Gordon shut the phone off.

'Was that Terry?'

Gordon grimaced without replying.

'Why won't you talk with him?'

Again Gordon wouldn't answer.

'Did Terry have anything to do with Malc's accident?'

'Why would you think that?'

'Just from the questions the police were asking.'

'You didn't think that before.'

'The police asked more questions about Terry than they did about Malc.' Ian shrugged and looked out at the fortress apartments lining the South Thames, massive stone-clad blocks with sheer blank backs under which the smaller 50s housing estates looked pretty and quaintly poor.

Gordon drove in silence, thinking, his tongue-tip worrying his lower lip, considering, Ian thought, how to phrase what was on his mind.

'Malc,' Gordon began with a quick clipped cough, 'thinks that Terry pushed him. He can't remember the accident, but he's certain that Terry pushed him. The police have confused him, and keep feeding him ideas about his brother. And added to that he's started on a new medication. So one minute he's half asleep, and the next he's manic, believing everything that anybody tells him.' He rubbed his thumb across his brow. 'The police want him to press charges. Terry's done some stupid things, but he wouldn't hurt Malc.'

'What about that list? Why was Terry so worried about the police having Malc's list?'

Gordon shrugged. 'There's a restraining order stopping Terry from going anywhere near Jimmy outside of supervised times. So he's nervous. Any trouble would be playing into Janine's hands. She'd love nothing more than to take him back to court.'

'Maybe she has good reason to.'

'That's their business.'

'So what was Malc's list?'

Gordon slowly shook his head. 'Why don't you tell me what you think the list is about?'

'I've no idea, but Terry wouldn't do anything without telling you. And Malc wouldn't be able to keep his mouth shut.'

'And why would Malc tell me and not you?'

'Because it's something to do with those pills, isn't it? It's either a list of people they're buying from, or selling to.'

Gordon looked in the mirror, then, slowing the car down, he pulled over, stopping in the bus lane.

'Tell me how you worked that out.' Speaking in a deliberately calmed voice he looked directly at Ian. 'Tell me how you can turn a simple list of names into a drug cartel?'

Ian looked out at the road, wondering whose names were on the benefit cheques.

'I don't know.'

'Did you ask Malc what the list was?'

'I haven't seen him.'

Gordon stretched his arms over the steering wheel. 'You're beginning to sound like Malc. The list is nothing,' Gordon insisted. 'I know it's not what you want to hear, but it's nothing. A joke list made up in a pub. We came up with the names one night at the Britannia and Malc wrote them down. I don't even remember what it was for. Most of them are footballers. That's all it is. Nothing is going on. Those pills, I've said before, were nothing.'

'Why didn't you say earlier?'

'Would it have made any difference?'

Gordon parked next to the cinema on Islington Green and they walked briskly to Louise's, keeping close to the buildings. It was raining again and the road and pavement shone with a dull gun-metal lustre.

Outside Louise's squat a new set of railings recently painted with red oxide led into the courtyard. Tied to the railings was a banner: Cadugan Court. Dowling Construction/Islington Council. Partners in Community.

Dowling. The name soured in Ian's stomach. This was the same contractor that ousted them out of Hopewell. Gordon walked ahead, striding briskly up the stairs two at a time. The doors to the rubbish chutes were gone and the stairwell stank. There were dust-sheets loose on the concrete steps, and on the first landing the graffiti was painted over in mismatched blocks of grey paint.

The flat beside Louise's was still occupied. Rough and dirty blankets were pressed against the windows, taped to the door was a hand-painted sign protesting against the development.

There was no front door to Louise's flat; it was clear that she was gone. The bath, sinks, and toilet were removed and the electricity cables were routed from the wall, dug out from the plaster. The windows were open in the back room and the larger panes broken. Shards of glass littered the floor reflecting the last of the day's light up on to the walls. Outside the city fell away to a vale of tightly packed offices and low-rise estates. Immediately behind the flats, set back to back, was a long office building built of modular units cast in white concrete, the windows tinted gold, masking the interior. With a quick huff Gordon said that it was the North London Police Headquarters. Ian asked again when Gordon had last heard from Louise, and he replied that it was two days, perhaps three.

'She didn't mention anything about moving?'

Gordon set his hands on his hips and shrugged, shaking his head.

'Why would she leave without telling us?' There was a small measure of blame in Ian's voice. Louise, the most resilient of the three, had now been hounded out of two houses, and all the while there were vacant rooms above every single one of Patterson's shops.

Gordon was out of cigarettes. He prowled around the house, restless and irritated, unable to settle. Picking up his coat he suggested that they go to the Britannia, saying that there was time for a quick drink before they called last orders. Ian was tired, and the Britannia, he said, was the last place he wanted to go to. Terry would be there, and he didn't want to see him. Gordon picked up his jacket, and then asked with studied casualness if Ian had seen that policeman around?

Ian asked 'around what?' and 'which policeman?' knowing exactly what Gordon was asking.

'The one that was asking after Terry.'

Ian shook his head.

'Terry saw him at the Britannia.' Gordon clicked his fingers, recalling a name, 'Sutcliffe. Neil Sutcliffe.' He held his arm half-in, half-out of the jacket sleeve. 'He was at the Britannia the other night. He left just before you did.'

Ian shook his head again. 'Who's Sutcliffe?'

'The policeman looking into Malc's accident. Terry said he was watching us.'

'Where?'

'The other night. At the Britannia.'

'So?'

'He was watching us.'

'So?'

'Terry saw you talking with him. Outside. He said you walked away together.' Ian scratched his palm anxiously.

Gordon slowly nodded. 'I told him he was wrong.'

Ian counted the cigarette stubs in the ashtray beside his feet. 'He wasn't wrong.' His voice was assured, quiet, but assured. 'I did talk with someone, but it wasn't the policeman.'

Gordon's jacket caught at his shoulders.

'He isn't the policeman. He looks like him, but it's not the same person.'

'You just said you didn't talk with him?'

'I didn't talk with the policeman, I talked with someone else. Someone who looks like him.'

'But you were talking with him.'

Ian looked up at Gordon. 'I went home with him.'

Gordon softly cleared his throat. 'You went where?'

Ian shook his head. 'I went back with him to his house.'

Gordon looked away. 'What did you go to his house for?'

Ian curled up, and asked Gordon how explicit did he want him to be?

Ian sat up until one o'clock waiting for Gordon to return, going over and over the conversation, stunned that that was it.

Underlying his anxiety was the more pungent truth that he had lied to Gordon for almost as many years as he'd known him.

Deciding to sleep on the couch, Ian found Gordon's sleeping bag tucked under the bed. As soon as he lay down the telephone rang. Ian listened as the machine caught the call. It was Shannon, Gordon was at the Max-Factory, a nightclub at Surrey Docks. He was drunk, and he was getting belligerent. Was he there?

Ian picked up and asked what, exactly, was Gordon doing?

Shannon gave a little laugh. 'Well, he isn't dancing.'

Gordon was starting to cause trouble. She could get him a taxi, but doubted that he would go unless someone was with him, and she didn't want to be responsible. Ian asked if she had any money; Shannon reluctantly said yes, and Ian reminded her that she was the one asking for the favour.

Ian could hear the music from the club even before he was out of the taxi. A dull and rapid pulse. A scattering of people smoked and squabbled outside, and Shannon waited, smoking beside the black double warehouse doors.

Ian asked the driver to wait, and the driver started laughing. The man leaned round and speaking through the glass said that Ian should pay him first. 'How can I be sure you'll come back?' he asked, pointing at the meter. £11.40. It was fair enough, Ian thought, the man had a point.

Ian told him again that he didn't have any cash, and pointing towards Shannon, said that she was going to give him the money, that woman there, but first he needed to go inside to collect someone. 'Look. Here. I'll leave this.' Ian took off his sweater.

The driver shook his head and Ian held up his wrist. 'I'll leave my watch then?' Still the man shook his head.

'Jesus. What do you want?'

'Your shoes.' The driver broke into a very broad smile, nodding as he spoke.

'Give me your shoes. You'll be back.'

Ian took off his shoes, telling the driver that this just wasn't normal, and that he would remember his number, so he'd better wait.

Swearing as he walked, Ian hobbled across the gravel towards Shannon. Dressed in a stylized bicycle messenger's outfit, a black and yellow lycra suit cut off at the arms and thighs, she looked cold. Throwing her cigarette away when she saw Ian, she wiped her hands over her hips.

'It's all right,' she said, leading Ian past the bouncer and into the club.

The Max-Factory was a long and broad storehouse with breezeblock walls. The club was packed with a field of people hunched together, their heads and shoulders strafed by bare white and red lights. Even those not dancing could not help but move. Ian could not see where he was stepping, the concrete floor was cold and sticky and he worried that he would tread on glass. Black and yellow tape – police line, do not cross – spooled across the rafters, and racing bikes with their wheels and frames outlined with cords of smaller flickering lights hung from perforated I-beams. The entire space was painted black. On a catwalk edged with fluorescent tape, five women dressed exactly like Shannon danced under alternating spot-lights syncopated to a hard and driven rhythm.

'What took you so long?' She shouted as she hustled Ian towards the bar, nudging and pushing her way forward. Ian gripped her shoulder and said that she should try and find a cab at this time of night, and even though she was annoyed she managed a smile, and promised that she would not forget the favour. Once through to the bar she asked someone if she could use his seat. The man grinned at his friends as Shannon knelt up on his stool. Perched on the bar-stool she was only just over Ian's height, even without his shoes. Pointing across the dance floor, Shannon mouthed, 'Can you see him? He should be over there.'

Ian looked but could not find him.

Shannon slipped up to the bar and asked one of the bar staff. The man clapped his hand to his ear and then swept his hand along the bar and shrugged. There were too many people for him to have noticed.

'Useless.' Shannon waved wearily at the bar, and half-apologizing told Ian that she had to go. 'He can't have got far. Try the toilets.'

She pointed at the raised walk and mouthed before disappearing, 'Find him and get him out of here. I don't want any trouble.'

Ian could smell the toilets before he reached them. The floor was wet, as, consequently, were his socks. A line of young men stood at the urinals, sweat matting their shirts to their backs. Men smoked as they pissed, boisterous and rousty, or drunk, heads nodding with threat. Ian checked the stalls, and found Gordon in the last booth. The door was open, and Gordon sat inside, smoking, with his trousers buckled up, and his elbows on his knees. He was clearly drunk. Wearily registering a little surprise he asked Ian what he was doing here.

'Do you have any money?'

Gordon slowly checked his pockets, then handed his wallet to Ian, asking if he would get him something too.

'I'm taking you home.'

Pointing at Ian's feet, Gordon asked what he was doing coming out with no shoes on?

As they left the club the five dancing women crossed their arms over their breasts and snapped their hips forward, fucking at the air. The music was a single deep blare, and Ian squinted at the walkway searching for Shannon, but he could not tell her apart from the other dancers.

Gordon's head lolled back as Ian steered him towards the door.

'Lovely,' he said. 'Lovely. Now tell me you don't like that.'

Ian left a bowl for Gordon beside his bed with some Dettol in it. The smell made him retch, and he forgot for a moment that he was hungry. Returning to the couch Ian regretted that he hadn't taken up Gordon's earlier offer of a meal. Now everywhere would be closed and he would have to go hungry. It would have been a different evening, an evening he would have preferred. The street outside was dark and empty, and doubtless every sensible person was now in bed. Gordon belched in the hallway. Leaning heavily against the door he called softly to Ian.

'You awake?' He swung unsteadily into the room, and switched on the light, fumbling for a pack of cigarettes in his shirt pocket. 'Did you see Shannon?' He pulled a cigarette from the packet and dropped it on the floor. Picking it up, he grinned at Ian. 'She's seeing someone else.'

He lit the cigarette and held the match out to Ian. The match burned down to his fingertips. 'You could have talked to me before.'

Ian wanted to say that it never really mattered before and that it didn't matter now. 'There wasn't any reason to tell you.'

Puzzled, Gordon took the cigarette slowly out of his mouth. 'I knew. I already knew.' He tapped his forehead. 'What did you think I'd say? Do you think I didn't know?'

Ian shrugged, uncomfortable at Gordon's questions. 'Then what difference does it make?'

'It makes a difference.' Gordon rubbed smoke out of his eye. 'It makes a big difference.'

Gordon sat at the end of the couch, then flopped back, and closed his eyes. Ian took the cigarette out of his hand, then turned out the light, and followed the cat into the bedroom.

At Waterloo, running late, just passing the Old Vic and heading to work, Ian was struck by the slick black side of a taxi and whacked, head-over-heels, into the middle of the street. Suddenly down with his back flat to the tarmac, he looked up, blinking, breath hefted out of him, baffled, thinking *that's the sky, I'm looking at the sky.* As the taxi slid on, the passenger turned completely around, alarmed, her fingers splayed across the glass as if she too were falling.

Ian rolled on to his side, hugging his arm, trying to understand the accident. He had fallen against the taxi, right shoulder, right arm, his splint striking the glass before he tumbled over the crossbar. The splint was broken. Somewhere in the muddle, before the bike scuddered from under him, he heard the plastic break with a clear, fresh snap. The radio lay on the road, knocked out of its holster. Ian flexed his hand and reached for it, not minding that the bike was fucked, but Jesus, he couldn't afford to replace a radio. How much did those things cost?

The battery was still in the holster and it took him a while, slowly rising to his knees, to find it. A tingling ache sheered down his left leg, hip to heel, a roll of pain furring down the bone. He couldn't feel his backside, and there was a small circle of people around him.

A woman separated from the crowd and knelt beside him, asking if he was alright. 'I saw everything,' she said, scowling at the scrape on his cheek.

Grimacing, he clipped the battery back into the radio. A small crack ran diagonally across the battery housing. His left hand was grazed and sticky, and he felt sick, sicker at the damaged radio than the accident.

The radio light came on as soon as the battery was inserted, but the battery would not stay in its housing. Ian lay back and called in, asking for Dom, his fingers stinging and his hand shaking. Tiny beads of blood perspired from the graze on his fingertips, and he felt himself close to tears. He'd skinned his hand and hit his head and battered his arse, and doubted that he could stand.

A piece of paper was held too close to his face for him to read. 'It's the taxi.' The woman backed away and pointed at the station. 'That's the number of the taxi. They drove off.' Ian looked up into her face. Honestly concerned, the woman frowned back down at him, her hand reaching for his shoulder. She asked if he could stand. He should, she said, get out of the road. Ian did not want to be touched, and he crawled sideways towards the pavement away from the woman, then lay back, swallowed whole by a headache.

Aching and feeling foolish, Ian walked slowly up Waterloo Road. His front wheel was so badly buckled that it could not turn, and it was difficult to manage the bike on its back wheel with just one sore hand. A soldier in full uniform had helped him to his feet. The man had picked up his bike and waited as Ian collected himself. The soldier was sympathetic, and wincing at the graze on Ian's left cheek, said that his hotel was close, Ian could come to his room and clean up. The soldier's attention – his concern, his smooth shaved jaw, his coarse uniform – seemed raw and pornographic. But Ian dithered, then insisted that he should walk to work. The man had patted his back and asked him if he was sure.

Ian stood at a crossing, waiting for the lights, counting backwards. He looked back, but the soldier was gone. The radio crackled, and Dom's voice cut in and out asking Ian what was going on. Ian pressed the base of the battery into the radio and said that he was alright, that he had the driver's number, but he needed to clean up. His bike was in bad shape. Dom told him to stay where he was.

As Ian crossed the road the cars honked at him. Dom called and asked for the diameter of the front wheel. Ian answered then took the battery out of the radio and threw it into his bag.

Ian waited on Waterloo Bridge, shivering, leaning into a sharp wind, struggling to keep himself composed. He counted rapidly to himself, adding up sevens. People coming from the North Bank walked wide of him, and behind them, a full head and shoulders higher, he saw Peter, one hand on the handlebar of his bike, the other holding a spare wheel.

Setting his bike and the wheel against the parapet Peter asked Ian how he was, shouting above the wind. Why didn't anyone call the police?

Ian shook his head, concentrating on his counting, and let his bike fall into the road, caring less that a car could run over it. His fingers twitched in time with the numbers rushing through his head. Peter picked up the bike and set it on the pavement. Quickly looking it over, he spun the back wheel and checked the chain and gears. After assessing the damage he turned the bike upside down. He could fix it, he said. No problem. 'But what about you?'

Ian stopped counting and asked where the spare wheel came from? Peter explained that the courtyard behind Western was packed with bike parts. Peter nervously rubbed Ian's shoulders and asked again if he was alright. The scrape on Ian's cheek was beginning to swell and weep. 'You need to clean yourself up. Where do you hurt?'

Ian pointed at his head, his left hip, and held up his left hand. 'I landed on my back. I think I went head-over-heels.'

Peter looked into Ian's eyes and asked if he could see clearly?

Ian described the accident and then, cringing, asked Peter if the seat of his trousers was ripped. He turned around and lifted up his T-shirt. His hand trembled, with cold perhaps, or shock. His backside still prickled and his fingertips stang. Peter said that there was a small cut, but no-one would notice if he kept his shirt untucked.

'I think the radio's broken.'

Switching radios, Peter insisted that Ian sit down, and handing him his satchel he took out his tobacco, saying that Ian should help himself, there were cigarettes already rolled inside. Ian watched as Peter replaced the wheel. Peter's activity made him feel useless, and to occupy himself he fixed the broken splint back on to his forearm and began counting again.

'I think someone tried to pick me up.'

Peter paused from loosening the front hub nuts.

'A soldier. Said I could clean up in his room. Maybe I was confused.'

Once the wheel was changed, they exchanged bikes and returned to Waterloo Station. There was a small first-aid kit in Peter's satchel.

'Clean your face with cold water first. Otherwise you'll only start it bleeding.'

Taking both bikes Peter said that he would lock them together outside the station. Ian could go and clean himself in the toilets.

Ian walked wearily through the station; he felt weak and at each footfall his hip ached. Getting down the stairs to the lavatory was tricky, and he thought that he might fall. For the past few days he had been afraid of being hit by a car and having his arm crushed. Now that an accident had occurred he felt immune, relieved, and beaten.

The attendant, an old, skinny man, pushed the turnstile round for free and handed him a stack of paper towels, muttering to himself. A line of five or six men stood at the urinals. One by one they turned to look quickly at him, not wanting to stare but suspecting perhaps that he were a drunk or a lout. Beside the turnstile was a long counter of steel sinks. Ignoring the men Ian shucked off his two T-shirts, pulling them wide over his head, and leaving them hanging, sling-like, over his right arm. Looking into the mirror he gave himself a wry grim smile, then leaned forward to assess the damage. The scrape on his temple and cheek puffed out a face already bloated with lack of sleep, and his hair stuck to the wound. He'd looked better, he thought, he'd also looked a lot worse. The irony wasn't lost on him, not six hours before Gordon had warned him that this would happen. Now, if they were still on talking terms, he would persuade him into another job.

Ian plugged the drain with paper towels and filled the sink with cold water. Inside Peter's bag was a bottle of surgical spirits and a pack of cotton wool pads, antiseptic salve, and a bandage. Dousing one of the pads with spirits he gingerly patted his temple. To his surprise the pad felt cool, and the harder he pressed the more it soothed the sore. The skin around the wound was gummy, pulpy, and numb. As he carefully cleaned out the dirt, the scrape began to weep a clear liquid. Cleaning his fingers and elbow was a different matter, and the spirit stung, numbing his fingers. Ian swore, shook his hand, and was surprised to see Peter waiting behind him, a paper cup in his hand. Either side of him men washed their hands, keeping their eyes to themselves.

'Stings?' Peter placed the tea on the counter.

'I can't stand any mess on me.' Ian drew a long breath, shaking his hand and pointing to his temple. 'Sticky.'

He held up his hand for Peter to inspect, admitting that he was having trouble cleaning himself with one hand.

Peter doused another cotton pad, and with one hand resting against Ian's cheek, he carefully swept the wound, gritting his teeth and wincing. 'Tell me if I'm hurting you.'

Ian asked if Peter had eaten garlic the night before. Peter apologized, saying that he made pasta for his sister, and Ian said that he didn't mean anything by it, and anyway it was faint and he liked it. Ian sipped the tea and grimaced at the sweetness.

'You have the number of the taxi?' Peter spoke loudly as if to assure the other men beside them.

'Not his licence, his cab number.'

Peter nodded sternly. 'Dom will tell the other riders, sometimes we come across them again.'

'And then what?'

Bending over, Ian steadied himself against the counter, feeling dizzy. Another man left the toilets. Ian breathed out, his breath softly whistling. The attendant watched them from the turnstile.

'I think I should take you home. We can leave the bikes and get a cab.'

Ian slowly straightened, frightened by the idea that Peter would come back to Gordon's.

'I can't.'

'Why not?'

'It's just not possible.'

Ian looked down at his right arm. His mouth strained and his cheek hurt, and the sweet tea on an empty stomach was making him feel sick. Pulling off the splint, the straps caught around his wrist. His fingers were too sore to tug the Velcro apart. Frustrated and indignant, he tugged at the splint, muttering with his chin down to his chest that it was a fucking useless arm. His fingers started to bleed again, scudding small, dark slicks across the plastic splint. He thumped his right arm and held it out, separate from his body, so that Peter could untangle the straps. Had he ever, Ian asked, in his whole life, met anyone as stupid and useless.

Peter removed the splint and lay it beside the sink. It was broken, he said, the plastic snapped in two.

Ian explained that his right shoulder hit the taxi first, then his right arm, and that the splint took the force of the blow, protecting his arm.

'I broke my wrist two years ago.' Peter took hold of Ian's right arm. 'I didn't go to the doctor until the next morning. By that time it was so swollen I couldn't rotate my hand.' Peter held out his right hand to show small red dimples either side of his wrist. 'I had pins coming out of my arm. It took a month longer than it should have to heal.' That was stupid, he said. Riding a trial-bike with no gears and no brakes was asking for trouble. Getting hit by a taxi was par for the course for a messenger. It wasn't smart and it wasn't stupid. It was one of those things. He asked if there was any pain in his hand or wrist, and Ian said no, the only injury was where the straps had chafed the skin. There was cream in Peter's satchel. It was just skin cream, he said, a salve, it didn't smell of anything.

Peter carefully massaged Ian's forearm, his hand reaching easily, fingers to thumb, around Ian's wrist. Ian held his breath and watched Peter's face. Unlike every other person, Peter never asked about the arm, and his expression betrayed no abject curiosity or disgust. Catching their reflection in the mirror, Ian pulled away, aware that other men were watching.

Unbuttoning his shirt, Peter offered it to Ian, suggesting that he tie it around his waist to cover the tear in the back of his trousers.

'If you ever get stuck for somewhere to stay, I can put you up.'

As they left the bathroom the attendant pointed at Ian and told Peter to look after him.

They sat together on the concourse for almost an hour and Peter rested his arm round Ian's shoulders, holding him close, watching people waiting for trains. Ian turned his head to face the magazine stalls and photo-booths, counting the queues, embarrassed by Peter's unassuming tenderness.

Dom turned his chair fully around as Peter and Ian came down the stairs.

'So how is he?' Dom asked, his tone edging between sincerity and sarcasm.

'Alive at least.'

He beckoned Ian forward and sneered at his swollen cheek, asking how hard did he hit his head? Ian muttered that it was a hard knock, but probably not hard enough. As small as the scrapes were on his fingers he did not want to look or think about them.

Peter explained the accident, describing in detail Ian's tumble over the handlebars. Everyone agreed that it could have been worse. Derek insisted on getting the taxi's number.

Dom drew his chair back to his desk, making it clear that everyone should return to work. 'If you're up to it, you can help me with the telephones.'

Derek quickly stood up. 'If you stay here,' he smiled, 'then I can go out.'

Dom told Peter he had a run for him, and Peter picked up a new battery. Without explaining himself Peter reached into Dom's drawer and pulled out a roll of black electrician's tape and ran a length under the radio to hold the battery in.

Dom looked sideways, first at Ian, and then at Peter.

Despite Ian's misgivings, working with Dom was easy, and for much of the morning they were busy. Ian answered the phone and wrote down on a docket the client's name, what the package was, where it was going, and whether the delivery was standard or urgent. Dom took the dockets, made a note for billing – cash or account – and assigned the pick-ups to the riders. Sometimes the callers requested specific riders, Derek and Peter were the most popular messengers. Sometimes there were complaints, crude attempts to get a complimentary delivery.

'Why are the people who can most afford it always the ones who complain?' Dom asked, not particularly interested in an answer.

The phones stopped ringing at one o'clock. Unbothered, Dom turned on the radio and took out his cigarettes.

'Workers' play-time,' he said, smiling at his cigarette.

Dom ate all day, steadily and slowly, nibbling first on a packet of ginger snaps, then on dry crackers. There was always a plate in front of him. When he smoked, he pushed his chair back and had two or three cigarettes in a row, then pulled himself back wheezing to the desk to take a couple of aspirin. Although he didn't talk much and didn't encourage it, Ian imagined that he would rather have company than not. Dom commented on every job as it came in, recalling in every instance the caller's name, their company, and address, complete with pick-up details if the business was difficult to find. He was able to plot complex routes through the city, linking pick-ups for multiple deliveries, and Ian began to understand Peter's loyalty: Dom's knowledge of the city and his ability to keep all eleven riders active was, without doubt, astounding.

They listened to the radio as the narrator described an early map of Europe, a pictogram of a pilgrim's journey from London to Canterbury to Jerusalem. Ian told Dom that he remembered the map from a history or geography book at school. He remembered the countries as the narrator described them, their shapes approximate but familiar enough to recognize, all grouped around the Mediterranean. The pilgrim's route was marked out in days' lengths; occasional cities, cathedrals, shrines, and sepulchres were drawn as landmarks along the way. Beyond the reaches of the known world were sketched imagined lands, populated with a jumble of lepers, freaks, and monsters: men with dog-heads and ears large enough to sleep in; cannibals with single legs or scaly amphibian skin, idiot faces embedded in their stomachs; and women with triple breasts and bird-like beaks to suckle nectar; all curious and outlandish aberrations. Every one of these peculiar creatures kept as distant as possible from the real and plottable world by the mountains, forests, marshes, and stalwart city walls. At school Ian understood that the map represented a kind of apartheid; the civilized world did not include him or people like him. Any kind of physical absence, difference, or infirmity, however slight, was godless, an example to others to be feared, pitied, and abhorred.

Dom turned off the radio, telling Ian to run an errand for cigarettes. Beside the telephone was a freshly opened packet, but Ian welcomed the break. His leg ached and his arm felt stiff. Dom picked up the phone and cleared his throat, telling Ian to take a while.

As he left the cellar Ian heard Dom ask for a ward, and it was only when he was hobbling along the street that he understood that Dom was calling a hospital.

The afternoon was quiet, and time passed unevenly. Working in a small room without natural light, Ian had no sense of what was happening outside. Dom's days, he thought, must be very much like each other. He still wore Peter's shirt, tied tightly around his waist.

At three forty, Dom looked up at the clock. Hank-the-Wank was five minutes late.

They both looked expectantly at the telephone and sure enough, it started to ring. Dom answered, and twirling his pencil in his hand, Ian guessed that it was Hank-the-Wank.

After hanging up Dom pushed the microphone to Ian. Pointing at the two buttons, in and out, each marked with tape, he told him to make the call. This was Peter's run.

Peter stuttered with surprise, pleased to hear Ian's voice, and asked how he was. Ian replied quickly, saying that he was fine, knowing that he should not chatter.

'Later then.'

Two minutes later Peter called from a public telephone outside the Old Bailey, not wanting to talk over the radio for the other riders to hear. There was a pub, he said, the Station, literally an old ticket office straddling the railway lines on Denmark Hill. His sister knew the place, and if Ian was interested he could ride with him and they could go for a drink.

Ian said that it was too far out of his way, but Peter insisted. It wasn't any trouble, he said, and anyway, he was curious about the pub.

*

As the booths and tables were full they stood beside the bar, bounded on either side by businessmen, most of them in suits with their jackets off and sleeves rolled up.

Peter's mood thickened, outwardly there was no visible or obvious sign of change, but conversation between them became awkward, and it was apparent that he was uncomfortable.

'Do you go home much?'

Peter asked what he meant.

'Do you ever go back to Ireland?'

Peter placed his beer back on the counter. Pensively sucking his upper lip he shook his head. No. He hadn't been back to Ireland since he left school. He wasn't Irish, he went to boarding school in a small village outside of Dublin for nine, ten years, a long time ago. London was home now. 'I was born in Durban, South Africa.'

The noise around them was so erratic that it sometimes swallowed Peter's words and sometimes left him shouting. 'I haven't lived there since I was eight. I was sent to school in Ireland because that's where my mother's family come from. They moved to Rhodesia when they were first married, moved to South Africa in the Sixties, then came over to Britain ten, or fifteen years after that, when I was finishing school.'

'So are you South African?'

Peter smiled uncertainly, and answered, 'British, both of my parents are British.' Everyone commented on his accent, but for good or bad he was stuck with it.

'So you haven't been back since you were eight?'

'No.'

'Have you seen much of your parents?'

'They live in High Wycombe. My father just retired as a civil engineer.'

'Do you remember Africa?'

'No. Not really.'

Ian stood away from the bar, nursing his pint, trying not to be jostled. Running the figures through his head, he guessed that Peter was one or two years older. Not knowing what to say, he asked Peter if he liked boarding school, and Peter shrugged softly.

'You didn't feel dumped?'

'It wasn't like that.'

Ian looked for some sign of how to react, but Peter's expression gave nothing away, except perhaps resignation.

'I wanted to go to boarding school, just to get away. I lived in the same house for fifteen years. I've been around the same people, more or less, since I could walk and talk. We went to the same schools, the same pubs, did the same odd jobs, signed on at the same dole office. It felt like everything changed after school, but most of the people who went on to college came back. And they're all still there. Not that I properly know any of them except Gordon.'

Peter took out a five pound note and held it up. A tip from Hank-the-Wank. His pint was still half-full on the counter behind him. The group beside them clapped and cheered. 'I can't stay much longer. I don't have any lights.'

Ian said that it didn't matter. Gordon would not be home and Peter could come back if he wanted.

Peter leaned forward, puzzled, his elbow threatening to nudge back his beer. Ian repeated his offer.

'Let me make sure he's not home.'

Peter gently nodded, his eyes deep and fixed on Ian's mouth.

The telephones were back beside the toilets, set between the doors. Ian waited for the answering machine and looked back at the bar. With one foot on the brass rail, Peter faced the mirror behind the counter, his hands set lightly on the wooden curve, waiting to be served. The answering machine picked up, and Ian caught Peter's reflection. His expression was unwavering, bare, honest and vulnerable; and with a small shock he realized that Peter understood the offer of a place to stay to mean much more than he intended.

Ian returned to the bar with a shallow shy smile. Peter was

still waiting to be served, and they awkwardly agreed that they should leave.

The night air was cold and the street wet, and as they walked their bikes down Denmark Hill Ian held his breath and kept in step with Peter, worried that Gordon might be home, or worse, that he would arrive in the middle of the night and find them together in his bed. He slowed to a halt as they turned in to Vicarage Grove. Pretending to search for his keys, he checked for Patterson's car. There were no lights on in the house. His mouth was dry and he was relieved to find the house empty. Peter stood close beside him as he unlocked the door, suddenly intimate.

Ian called up the stairs and the cat answered with a faint mew.

'I hope you like cats.'

Peter said that he wasn't hungry.

Ian reached for the light-switch, forgetting that the bulb was burned out. Looking up the dark stairwell he felt a vague sense of dread. What was he thinking bringing Peter back to Gordon's? By the time they had brought their bikes up to the landing his mind was changed about sleeping with him.

It was hard to pick a reason. Cold feet? Nerves? Uncertainty? Guts of feathers, he thought, I can't do it here. I can't fool around in Gordon's house, least of all in his bed. It would, he thought, be different in a club or sauna, a place securely distant from family. Besides, Ian did not doubt that Gordon would find out, something would give them away, and he would know exactly what they were doing.

'I'll make us some tea.'

Spooked at company, the cat hurtled chaotically from room to room. Peter followed after her and brought her back. Her legs stuck out and paddled as he forced her down to his lap.

'What was that cartoon with the skunk?'

'*Pépé le Pew.*'

Peter ran his hands firmly up the cat's back, from tail to head, ruffling her fur. The cat stuck her backside up, purring loudly, drunk with the attention. 'She's like the cat that gets paint on her back. The one that gets chased all the time.'

Making tea was a formality, and something for Ian to do. He set the cups parallel to the draining-board, nestled together but not touching, the handles turned away from each other. He thought about sex all the time, imagining himself with almost everyone he met. Why then was this so difficult? Every day Ian would look at people on the street, on the bus or the train, and wonder what that person, male or female, would be like in bed. He looked for signs in how they dressed or behaved, and wondered if anyone ever thought of him in that manner, and what they might suppose. What was it that his body told them?

The milk was sour, congealed and heavy in the bottle. Ian asked if Peter minded having his tea black, and Peter said that he wasn't particularly thirsty.

Ian wondered what was supposed to happen. Technically he knew what was what, but he couldn't picture it, not with Peter, and he thought again of the doctor, and how easy it was to have sex with people that he did not know. He needed to think, and he couldn't think with Peter sitting there.

Ian folded up a sweater for a pillow and pulled out the sleeping bag, labouring his decision to sleep on the couch in the front room. Peter stood in the doorway, baffled, scratching the back of his neck.

'You don't have to give up your bed.'

'I usually sleep on the couch. You're welcome to the bed.'

Peter attempted to protest, but Ian insisted.

'It's Gordon's bed. I wouldn't feel comfortable.'

For a moment Ian thought that Peter understood. Bundling up the sleeping bag, he quickly said good-night and began to make his bed on the couch.

*

The doors to both rooms were open. Ian listened as Peter undressed and settled into Gordon's bed. He sat with the sleeping bag drawn over his shoulders, feeling angry, intensely angry at himself, numbers catching in his head.

The house became still, and he sat for a long time staring hard into the dark doorway until the blackness itched and the silence pressed into his ears. Outside, a long way off, he could hear buses idling at the traffic lights.

Rising slowly and quietly he crept cautiously into the hall and stood close to the wall beside Gordon's open door. He breathed through his mouth, hoping that Peter could not hear him, his pulse catching in his throat. In the darkness he could see Peter's clothes scattered on the floor at the end of the bed. One step further, he thought, and he would be committed. One step.

Peter coughed and called softly for Ian.

Once, twice, and again. A soft whisper.

Ian woke early, wide awake and alert from the moment he opened his eyes. Peter was also awake, and Ian could hear him shuffling around in Gordon's room. His doubts about the night before, his indecision, now seemed foolish, and he hoped that Peter hadn't heard him creeping around in the corridor.

Gordon's door squeaked lightly, and the cat jumped off his thighs and ran mewing to the doorway. Ian turned carefully on to his side; Peter crouched at the door, fully dressed, gently shushing the cat, a low early sun striking his face.

Unable to keep still, Ian pretended to wake, and was disappointed to see that he was alone. From the corridor he could hear the sound of Peter wheeling his bike to the stairs. Disappointment pressed him deeper into the couch.

Once the front door closed, he hurried to the window and ducked down. Already on his bike, Peter glanced up at the house and was gone. Swearing at himself, Ian crawled into Gordon's bed and pulled the covers entirely over his head. The sheets were cold and there was no sign that Peter was ever there.

Gordon returned home at eight o'clock. Ian lay in bed listening to him walk through the house. After ten minutes Gordon leaned into the room and softly asked Ian if he was awake. In his hands were some of Ian's books. His hair was freshly cropped, and he was clean-shaven, the goatee gone, making his face softer, younger, and unfamiliar.

'I'm up. I'll put these in the front room.'

Ian sat up squinting, a little bad-tempered.

'What happened to your face?'

'I was hit by a taxi.'

'Jesus. Have you seen yourself?' Gordon hesitated, weighing the books in his hand, uncomfortable in his own bedroom. He took the books to the front room and returned to the bedroom with Ian's splint.

'I'm throwing this away.'

Ian said that he intended to fix it.

'I'm throwing it out. You've been told you don't need it. You should be doing those exercises and the swimming, like you were told. This is stopping it from getting any stronger.'

Ian slipped out of bed and took the broken splint out of Gordon's hands. He dropped it on the floor, on top of his clothes.

'I'm trying to tidy up.'

'I'll get out of your way then.'

Ian picked up his splint and clothes. Pushing past Gordon he said that he was going to work.

'I'll tell you this, but it isn't to go any further,' Gordon followed after him. Terry, he said, had been working a small scam with Patterson's houses. He was signing on under at least five different names using Patterson's houses as addresses.

Ian leaned back into the hall. 'Where?'

'Deptford and Surrey Docks. That I know of. It's possible he's been doing the same in Leicester and Kettering.'

'How did you find out?'

'I asked Malc. Letters have been sent to some of the houses. He hasn't signed on for six weeks. As far as I can tell he was claiming both rent and unemployment. From the letters I've seen, I doubt that he's been paid anything.'

'So what are you going to do?'

'Nothing. It's a small thing, and it's finished with.'

Ian bought a twelve-inch metal ruler and a roll of gaffer tape from W.H. Smith on the Walworth Road. Sitting on the kerb, he repaired the splint. It wasn't pretty, but it would do. He thought about what he would say to Peter. A simple explanation, he thought, a simple apology, nerves, would explain it. It would be embarrassing but he knew that Peter would understand.

Ian practised what he would say on the ride in, but as he locked his bike he lost his nerve. It was, he thought, going to be difficult to explain. It was all so stupid. Checking the bikes locked together outside the Methodist Hall, he could see that Peter had not yet arrived.

Ian was later than usual, and the office was full. Sitting on a chair at the bottom of the stairs he waited, ready to catch Peter before he came down into the office.

At nine fifteen Dom began to hand out the jobs, starting the usual scurry for radios and batteries. As Dom handed a sheaf of dockets to Rhino he muttered that they were without Peter today, so everyone would have to keep on their toes.

Ian was kept till last. Dom handed him a docket, saying that the job was a 'wait and return'. Squinting at the graze on Ian's cheek he asked if he felt any better.

'No headaches or anything?'

'No. Did Peter say he was sick?'

Both Dom and Derek shrugged, neither thought that his absence was unusual.

Ian hesitated, wanting to ask more, but Derek was already at the door and Dom was busy on the phone.

At three thirty Ian sat in a hallway looking into William Hanker's office in Lincoln's Inn Fields. He felt doubly wretched, for being the cause of Peter's absence, and for profiting by taking his jobs. Outside a man sat on a small tractor drawing behind it a heavy steel roller over the flat broad plate of grass. It was, he thought, entirely the wrong time of year to be rolling or cutting grass.

Hank-the-Wank was younger than Ian expected. He had imagined a small and skinny old man with thinning hair and heavy spectacles. But William Hanker was broader and slightly taller than Ian, impeccably dressed in a suit and a striped tie, his hair clipped and combed and divided with a clean, knife-like parting.

Setting his papers in order, the lawyer rose slowly from his desk and strode the whole length of his office, soundlessly stepping across a soft ochre carpet, only to close his door.

As Ian waited Derek called to remind the riders that their cheques were ready. If they returned their dockets by four fifteen, Dom would pay them for the full week.

Back at Endell Street the riders grouped on the pavement unlocking their bikes. Ian was the last rider home, and Derek greeted him with a slow hand-clap. 'Back before five.' Dom tartly pursed his lips together. 'It must be Friday.'

Dom sighed as he nudged his chair forward. Ian's cheque lay almost unseen under his hand.

'I kept track of your jobs today. So you're up to date. How did you like your week?'

There was a cold tone in Dom's voice, perhaps dismissal. Ian's hand wavered at his cheek, fingers lighting on the graze.

'I like it. I know I'm slow.'

Dom smiled down at his desk and said that he would see him on Monday then.

'If you have Peter's cheque I could take it to him.'

'He picked it up himself.'

Ian walked to the stairs crestfallen. Derek followed behind him.

'Your cheque. Don't forget your cheque.'

Returning to the desk, Ian asked for Peter's address, explaining feebly that they'd talked about doing something that weekend.

Derek wrote down the address on a docket, saying that it was close, in fact, it wasn't very far at all.

Up on the street Ian opened the envelope and took a quick look at his pay cheque. Two hundred and sixty-seven pounds. Close to three hundred pounds. The figures ticked through his head. Three hundred pounds. Enough for an air-fare to somewhere sunny, to some beach where he could go and shove his stupid timid head into the sand. The money, he thought, solved old problems, and last week he would have been glad of it. But money would not help him with his new troubles.

Ian stopped at the chippie on his way back from the station on Denmark Hill. There was little comfort in returning to the pub he'd visited the night before with Peter, but there was a slender chance, he thought, that Peter might show up. He ate the chips sitting on Gordon's steps, the vinegar smarting his lips, thinking of the many suppers he'd eaten waiting for Gordon to finish one thing or another.

Patterson's blue Jaguar was parked at the end of the street. Gordon's promise that the coast would be clear by closing time was already broken, but Shannon was working at the Max-Factory and would have to be gone by midnight. Obviously the job wasn't done. It was clear, Ian thought, that Gordon didn't want her, but he didn't want Shannon to say that it was over either, and one evening of sex and kindness, he thought, would be enough to persuade her to stay – at least until he could decide that she should go. It was mean and calculating, Ian thought, he'd done it before, a number of times, and besides, Peter might have called and they were keeping him out of the house. How is it, he wondered, that you can fill your head so rapidly, and so full of someone?

He'd called Peter before leaving the pub. A woman, his sister, answered and said that she hadn't seen him, but he was possibly out with some friends. The pub was loud, and he might not have heard correctly, but the news was discouraging. Peter had few friends at Western, and he'd never mentioned anyone else. It was a miserable end to a miserable day. Two days before he'd thought of Peter as nothing more than a considerate man and a decent cyclist, but today everything he saw brought him to mind.

Gordon's sleeping bag was set on the couch and his bedroom door was firmly closed. The cat stood sentry outside, staring up at the handle. Shannon's coat was laid carefully across the seat next to the window. Ian stretched out on the floor watching the television with the sound turned down, unable to make himself comfortable. There were no messages on the answering machine. It was disappointing that there was no word or message from Peter. The screen's blue light flickered across the coat. After a while Ian curled under the sleeping bag, and the cat settled on his chest. Unable to sleep, he imagined Peter's body, but he could not clearly picture his face.

Midday and Gordon was out, his jacket gone from the banisters and the house left quiet and cold and empty. Ian dressed in the hallway, anxious not to waste the day. It wasn't that he was thinking too much about Peter, he told himself, he just wasn't thinking enough about other things. The pockets and seams of Gordon's jeans were still damp, and he dressed with some difficulty. On the floor beneath the radiator was a note from Gordon. A man had called for him late yesterday afternoon, but didn't leave his name. Ian hurried to the answering machine and saw that one new message had been left while he was taking a shower. He didn't doubt that the call was from Peter, but even so, he was still surprised to hear his voice.

The message was clear and simple. Peter said he would be home all day if Ian wanted to call him back. He would like to hear from him. Ian played the message a third time, leaning against the banisters and smiling to himself.

Dom, he guessed, would have given Peter his number.

Ian did not know what to do, he should, he realized, call Peter, but he was never comfortable talking on the telephone, and Peter would read his awkwardness as something else, and they would be no further ahead than they were two nights before. It would be better to go to his house, see him face to face, and if he wasn't in, then that would be an answer or a solution of sorts.

11 Hunter's Close, N1

Ian stood at Peter's door staring at the black paint, worrying about what he should say. A new doubt troubled him – what if Peter was with someone else? He knew that it was unlikely, but the idea made him wretched. It would be easier to leave.

He raised his fist, ready to knock. Dissatisfied with the speed at which he raised his arm, he thought that he should knock on the count of five. Counting as he raised his arm, he wasn't sure if the two knocks should come on the four and the five, which meant raising his arm in three; or if the knock should come after, on a six and seven? Stepping back on to the pavement, he took a breath and looked around, feeling stupid and anxious. Five, or seven? The street was empty, unnaturally so, he thought.

Stepping briskly up to the door, he knocked hard. No counts. He listened as another door opened deep inside the house, whispering five, five, five, five, five. A slight suck of air pulled at the front door, rattling the letterbox. Ian held his breath.

Peter opened the door and stepped back, astonished, as if it were impossible that Ian could be there. Hiking his thumb over his shoulder he sputtered, 'I just called you.'

Without hesitating Ian stepped forward, cupped one hand around Peter's neck and kissed him.

They kissed, shyly, delicately, air pocketed between their mouths. From back inside the house came the high and dissonant shriek of a kettle. They separated and kissed again.

Peter shoved the door shut with his heel, and Ian leant into him, his cheek pressing against Peter's neck as they held tightly to each other. Ian whispered that he was glad to see him, and that they should talk. Peter nodded and they separated reluctantly, both looking down, neither knowing what to do with their hands.

'Kettle.' Peter grinned and scratched the back of his neck, then pointed over his shoulder.

'Where can I put my bike?' Ian's voice sounded deceptively impassive.

Peter stood aside, holding the door open as Ian fetched the bike and brought it into the hall. They stood awkwardly together, both resisting the urge to fall into each other's arms again. Peter hugged himself to show that he was cold, and then pointed up the stairs.

Peter's room was a shambles, clothes and magazines littered the floor; socks lay where he'd dropped them. His bike sat upside down beside a small cabinet, tools and parts arranged in a particular order in an open drawer. He quickly picked up his clothes then stood suddenly lost in the middle of the room, his arms full. Now what to do? He opened a cupboard and thrust everything inside.

Neither of them knew what to say, and Ian began to think that he was acting too rashly, and that Peter was deliberately resisting him. A painful hollow yawned in his stomach and throat. Their first kiss was a disappointment. Abbreviated, clipped, without a proper beginning or end, it was just an open mouth.

Peter brushed his hand down Ian's arm and said that he was making tea, unless Ian wanted coffee, and that he would bring it up and they could talk.

Left alone, Ian sat on Peter's bed. This is his bed, he thought, slipping his hand under the sheets, this is where he sleeps. He looked around the room feeling hopeless. The walls were covered with clippings from magazines, pictures of cyclists and photographs, Ian supposed, of his family. In one he recognized Derek with his arm around Peter's shoulders, both of them smiling; behind them was a field filled with tents. Above the headboard was a 1997 calendar for the Tour de France, a team rounding a corner in the Alps, their bikes sheering in an acute angle, improbably stopped by the photograph. Beside Peter's bike was a small blue metal workman's cabinet on casters. On top of the cabinet was a pile of rags flecked with black circles from polishing, and a piece of paper with a telephone number but no name. The bike's gears lay disassembled on a sheet of newspaper, each part cleaned. The kiss was reserved, tender or respectful, he could not decide. After so much confusion he had expected some urgency, some fervour.

Peter returned carrying a tray, ridiculously full and clattering, stacked with a sugar bowl, packets of Digestives and Rich Tea biscuits, and three cups, one containing milk. He set the tray on the floor, and settled on his haunches beside it.

Asking what Ian wanted to talk about, Peter leaned over the tray, pouring milk into both cups. When Ian did not answer he asked if he was seeing anyone.

Ian coughed and said no. Peter poured the tea.

'So you and Gordon. You're not a couple?'

Ian sat forward to take the cup. 'I've known Gordon since I was nine. He has a girlfriend. We've always had separate friends.' Stirring sugar into his tea, Peter brushed his hair back.

'So you're not a couple then?'

Ian set down his cup, and began to explain that Gordon was raised by his grandmother, Mrs Marshall, whose house on Porter Road backed on to theirs. Mrs Marshall worked evenings at Markwicks, printing bingo tickets and wedding announcements, and Ian's mother worked days, first for the DHSS and later for a Prestons bakery. Gordon's grandmother looked after them during the day, and Ian's mother looked after them in the evenings. It was an arrangement between their families. That was all it was. Half standing, Peter apologized, saying that he was only asking, it wasn't any of his business, and they kissed again in short, dry pecks. Ian whimpered with frustration, and feeling strangely distant, thought that he sounded ridiculous.

They lay together on Peter's small bed with the covers pushed back, and their shirts shoved up. Their jeans, pants and socks were rolled into a ball at their feet. Peter's body was long and pale and slender, with narrow shoulders and a small waist, his thighs disproportionally thick and developed from cycling. Apart from the tough hanks of black and wiry hair at his armpits and crotch, his body was almost hairless. Peter glided his hand so softly over Ian's skin that sometimes they barely seemed to be touching.

Ian stood in the bath, his hand wavering over his thighs. Peter drew the curtain around them, feet squeaking on the enamel. The water, he said, turning on the shower, would run hot for as long as they wanted. Reaching for the soap, Peter quickly cleaned his armpits and groin.

'Stinky,' he smiled, stepping in and out of the stream, his hair stuck flat to his forehead. 'You have to tell me what you like.' Suds ran down his stomach and thighs.

'I like this.' Ian grinned back and rubbed his foot against the bath to repeat the sound that Peter had made.

Peter nuzzled into Ian's neck and they slipped together, arm in arm, pushing through the curtain, feet skidding on the wet bath. Peter attempted to right himself, but keeled clumsily forward, and they held on to each other, laughing.

Scrambling out first, Peter lay a towel across the side of the bath, and, telling Ian to sit on the towel, began to dry him. Ian watched his reflection in the bathroom mirror. Unused to what he could see, he was faintly startled, embarrassed. He was never comfortable naked, and whenever he saw himself it was always in parts, a face to shave, or an arm to massage. He avoided his reflection out of habit and here in a long slender mirror mounted to the back of the bathroom door was a whole picture, a complete body beside another complete body, uncovered by clothes or darkness. Studying Peter's face, he thought that they looked alike; both having pale skin and long boxy jaws and brows, and deep-set eyes. After two days Peter's beard was still only a faint and dirty smudge. How strange this was and how complete the change from only two hours before.

On a green glass shelf above the sink was a row of dense blue bottles of creams and conditioners and a number of smaller, squatter brown prescription bottles; the labels all made out for Peter. Following Ian's gaze, Peter looked up at the shelves, then turned suddenly. From downstairs came the clack of a door closing.

Ian closed his legs, and they both listened.

'My sister's home,' Peter whispered. 'I was supposed to make tea.'

Ian started to gather his clothes.

Peter's sister called up from the hall asking why there was a bike downstairs.

After a short silence they could clearly hear her coming up the stairs.

'Are you in there?'

'She's at the door,' Ian mouthed. Seeing his panic Peter started to laugh. His sister knocked on the door, a light double tap.

'You can't come in,' Peter called, 'I've got company.'

'How many today?'

'Five,' Peter answered, shoving his bare feet into his shoes. 'I'm serious. Don't come in.'

Peter stood with one hand ready on the door handle, the other on Ian's shoulder. Stroking Ian's back reassuringly, he opened the door. 'Jennah, Ian. Ian, Jennah.'

Leaning curiously into the room Peter's sister smiled and extended her hand. She was, she said, very pleased to meet him.

'I thought you were joking.'

Uncomfortable, Ian grinned stupidly. Jennah was slighter than her brother, and older, Ian guessed, by around ten years. Smartly dressed in a grey collarless business suit, with straight brown hair cropped cleanly at her shoulders, it was hard to find any similarity between them.

'What happened to the other four then?'

Peter pointed to the window.

Still smiling, Jennah made it obvious that she was appraising Ian. She avoided looking at his arm. 'Well at least you kept the handsome one.'

Peter laughed and agreed, and Ian waited, scratching his arm.

Jennah's accent, unlike her brother's, was faintly South African. Ian doubted that he would have guessed. Plummy and nasal, it would be ugly, he thought, if it were more pronounced. Stumbling to breach an awkward gap, Ian said that his sister was also called Jennifer.

'No, Jennah,' Peter corrected him, pronouncing his sister's name slowly, 'Jeah-na.' It was his grandmother's name, a family name. Ian apologized, saying that he had misheard.

Jennah asked Ian what his sister did, and Ian explained that she looked after her two children, twins. Smiling at her brother, Jennah said that her hands were probably full then.

'I have some wine.' Jennah stepped back out of the room, pulling the door closed behind her. 'Come down when you're ready.'

Peter raised his eyebrows and asked if Ian wanted to go downstairs. He rested his arms over Ian's shoulders and they kissed, falling naturally together.

They sat at the dining-room table. A bottle of red wine already open on the sideboard, and three glasses poured.

As Peter squeezed between his sister's chair and the sofa she reached for his hand and gave it a quick and affectionate squeeze. 'I've ordered Indian. I hope you don't mind.' She asked Ian if he liked working at Western, and Ian bumbled through his reply, saying that it was a good job as long as you remain on your bike. He began to describe his accident, and found it unnerving to have their undivided attention.

Jennah described a little of her day. She was working on a project which might soon be dropped, and she wasn't sure that it was worth the fight and bother necessary to save it. After a career in banking she had stumbled into journalism. Her expertise lay in properties and trusts. The banking world was no longer a club with limited and select entry, she said, speaking, Ian thought, as if none of it were true. Her habit of hooking her hair behind her ears reminded him of Louise. Finishing with a tidy smile, Jennah asked Peter if he liked the wine, and Ian if he would like another glass. Ian realized that he was drinking too fast. She was, he thought, as observant as his father.

Making her apologies, Jennah poured herself another glass and left to work in her office. Leaving the wine out on the table, she said that there was another half-bottle left over from the previous night if they were interested. 'I'll call you when the food arrives.' Ian watched her walk up the stairs. Except for

Peter's bedroom, everything in the house was Jennah's. The dark burgundy walls, the Indian silks, the thin black figurines of naked hunters set either side of the fireplace, the tapestry pillows and hardback books stacked beside the couch, and the plants set in an etched brass tray centred on the table, were evidence of modest and calculated taste. Pressed between the hyacinth bulbs were small ornaments, a collection of tiny white porcelain foxes.

Taking the wine with them, they returned to Peter's room and quickly undressed each other. Once naked Ian became nervous, and he sat at the end of the single bed with the quilt pulled over his thighs. Through the window he could see the silhouettes of the tops of trees and the backs of buildings at the end of Peter's garden. Small lights shone through curtained windows. Peter drew his hand down Ian's back, and asked what was it that made him change his mind?

Ian shook his head. It wasn't that he changed his mind, he said, Gordon's just wasn't the right place. It was difficult to explain. He caught himself, surprised by the contradiction; it wasn't too soon to sleep with Peter, but it was too soon to talk with any frankness. Reaching for his trousers he took out his wallet, drew out a photograph, and offered it to Peter.

The photograph showed two boys standing side by side in a garden: one, short, and with narrow shoulders and his arm in a sling, smiled awkwardly, squinting at the camera; the other, taller, and with no particular expression, stood with his hands in his pockets, appearing relaxed, perhaps distant. Behind them wind-blown foxgloves leaned into a plain brick wall. Ian could not remember the photograph being taken, but he could remember why his arm was in a sling. That was the summer spent at Sutton Hospital, and the last of four surgeries. It was also Gordon's first summer at Porter Road. Gordon appeared reserved and confident, the sun in his face and his hair forward over his eyes, a whole head taller than Ian.

'You wouldn't think we're almost the same age. Look how much smaller I am.'

Peter carefully studied the photograph and said that Ian looked uncomfortable. It was the clothes, they didn't fit him. Ian took back the photograph. The shorts were handed down from his sister, he remembered, and the baggy shirt and oversized sandals were Gordon's. Only the sling belonged to him.

'I learnt to tie my shoelaces that summer. I had to take the shoe off my foot to manage, but even so, it was a big day for the Proctor family.'

'Does he know about you?'

Ian shrugged and nodded, and Gordon loitered in his head, tiresome and exhausting.

They ate the left-overs from last night's supper for breakfast, sitting up in bed, and after, they horsed around on the floor surrounded by foil plates of dhal, saag paneer, and naan bread.

Pushing up the window, Peter leant against the painted sill. A dog barked and Peter barked back. Kneeling beside him Ian looked out over the gardens. The sun struck the wet slate on the roofs opposite. Shadows slanted across well-kept lawns. It was still early, a clear March morning, maybe eight o'clock.

'We should stay here.' Peter turned to face Ian. 'Just stay in this room.'

Turning back to the garden, he told Ian of his plans to travel through Turkey for two weeks at the end of April. 'Fly first to Athens,' he said, 'and then take the ferry.' He'd been to the Greek islands before, 'a big waste of time.' He'd also been to Crete, Malta, and Portugal on pre-season package tours. That way you were there before the rush, before everyone grew sick of tourists.

Conscious of his promise to Gordon to return to Amsterdam, Ian carefully agreed that it would be good to go somewhere. With just one week's wages he could now afford the holiday. He watched Peter as he looked down across the gardens. Confident and naked, his affection appeared certain; an undemanding and gentle intimacy. Ian had imagined something rougher, something more brutal.

Ian phoned Gordon from the kitchen while Peter fetched the Sunday papers. It was nearly midday and Jennah was out, working. Her cup sat alone in a clean sink. He wound the cord around his right wrist, the answering machine was switched off. Gordon picked up on the sixth ring.

'Where are you?'

'Islington.'

'Someone called for you yesterday.' Gordon's tongue clicked disapprovingly. 'Your Irish friend.'

'His name is Peter.'

'Is that where you are?'

Ian said that it was, and there was a long silence.

'Are you staying there?'

'What do you mean?'

'How long will you be staying there?'

Ian said that he didn't know, and again there was another silence.

'I'm missing the ledger I record the rents in. It was in the kitchen yesterday morning.' Gordon paused to cough. 'It was in the kitchen. On the table. It's gone now.'

Ian said that he hadn't seen it. This would end, he knew, in an argument.

'Only you and Terry have keys to the house.'

'Then Terry has it.'

'Terry was arrested yesterday morning.'

Ian asked what was going on, but Gordon would not answer. Ian repeated the question, and Gordon explained that Terry was picked up by the police on Saturday morning. He was in Deptford trying to cash one of the cheques.

'What cheques?'

'A benefit cheque. I've told you about this.'

'I thought you said it was over?'

'It is over. Terry has been arrested.'

Ian said that it didn't make sense, and Gordon replied that it was simple. There was nothing to understand. Terry was claiming unemployment benefit under different names. He was using Patterson's houses as addresses, and on Saturday morning he was caught trying to cash one of the cheques. 'I've told you this before.'

'He was signing on?'

'That's what I just said. I've told you this before.'

'Under different names?'

'Under different names.'

'How many houses?'

'What do you mean?'

'How many houses was he using?'

'I've already told you.'

'How many?'

'Three or four that I know of.'

'All in the same area?'

'More or less. I've told you this.'

'It doesn't make sense. If the houses are all in the same area, he'd have to sign on under all those names at the same benefit office. And he can't sign on under more than one name or they'd recognize him. What names was he using?'

'Does it matter?'

Ian ran the telephone cord through his fingers. 'They're the same people on Malc's list, aren't they? Did Malc have anything to do with it?'

Gordon paused. Ian could hear him light a cigarette. 'How did you come up with that?'

'Malc works in a benefit office.'

Gordon drew on his cigarette.

'He's a data-entry clerk. He manages payments! It wouldn't take much to change the accounts.'

'You're doing it again.'

'Doing what?'

'That thing where you make shit up out of nothing. Whatever Terry was up to, Malc had nothing to do with it.'

'Have you asked him?'

'What would I ask him for? It's perfectly simple. Terry signed on using other names.'

'It wouldn't work. You need Social Security numbers. You need a bank account, or you need a post office that will cash the cheques for you. They call up your past employers. I can't see Terry going to that amount of trouble for forty extra pounds a week. And besides, it's too much of a coincidence. Malc starts working on benefit payments and then his brother starts a benefit scam.'

'Ian. You're not listening.'

'You've picked up the cheques. I've seen them.'

'What cheques?'

'Terry's cheques. That night before we went to Louise's. You picked up two benefit cheques, you had them in the car. I saw them.'

'What of it?'

'Fine then. Don't tell me. Nothing's going on.' Ian looked out of the window, and thought about hanging-up.

There were nearly thirty people on Malc's list. As far as he knew Malc couldn't change the names and addresses on existing benefit claims, not without getting caught. It was more likely that he was introducing new claims to the database, adapting old records from accounts that were now closed. Ian did not know how possible this was. 'There were nearly thirty people on that list. That's nine hundred pounds a week, minimum.'

Gordon refused to answer.

'So what happens now?'

'What happens what?'

'Are you in trouble?'

'It has nothing to do with me.'

'You're responsible for Patterson's houses. If he was using those houses the police will want to talk to you.'

'It has nothing to do with me. Terry will have to see himself through this.'

'What about Malc?'

'What about him?'

'If he was involved then he'll be in trouble.'

Gordon gave a soft, frustrated groan. 'Ian. Have you talked to anyone?'

'About what?'

'About any of this. When you talked with the police, when they showed you that list, did you tell them where I live?'

'No. Of course I haven't. And anyway, they didn't show me the list.'

'What are you talking about?'

'The list. Malc's list. The police never had it.'

'What are you saying?'

'I'm saying I made it up to piss off Terry. Louise found it in Malc's pocket. She wrote a note on the other side saying that she was taking him to hospital.'

Gordon paused, and in a slow and careful voice he asked Ian to make himself perfectly clear. 'Have the police, at any time, ever seen the list of names?'

'No.'

'And you have it?'

'Yes.'

Ian could hear Gordon breathe out in one long smooth breath. 'Do you have any idea how much trouble you've caused?'

Backing up against the counter, Ian said that he should go.

He hung up the phone and then stared out over the sink, leaning against the fridge, his back flat to the cold metal door. Ian stared out at the flower pots hung beside the window, waiting for the counting to start, but nothing came. He did not know how long he could stay at Peter's, but it was clear that he should not return to Camberwell.

Peter returned with the Sunday papers and a packet of condoms. As they returned to bed Peter settled between Ian's legs making it clear that he wanted to fuck him; reaching into the bedside drawer he pulled out a tube of lube. There were hairs stuck to the snout. Ian was unsure, there was something inappropriately practical, perfunctory, about Peter's preparations, and the thought that it was planned irritated him.

Jennah returned in the early evening to find Ian curled up on the couch with Peter, watching *Songs of Praise*. Peter slept with his head resting on Ian's lap, locking Ian into the seat. Earlier in the afternoon they had made a half-hearted attempt to go out for groceries, but by the time they were dressed they realized that they would prefer to stay together and alone in the house, even if it meant that they would go hungry.

Kneeling beside Ian, Jennah asked if they had eaten. Ian shook his head.

Resting her hands on the arm of the settee, Jennah took off her shoes and rubbed her toes.

'What if I take you both out?'

Ian thought it would be rude to refuse, and Jennah tiptoed into the kitchen to call and book a table. There was, she said, a small Spanish place quite close that did an acceptable paella. Or did he fancy pasta? She read through the menu on the fridge door.

Light from the kitchen fell across Peter's face, and Ian was struck by how peaceful he looked.

On the television a round balding man stood on a wet and sober moor with a whole choir behind him. Ian recognized the music before the man opened his mouth. It was a sickly parlour song that his mother once sang.

The man clasped his hands, and as he sang his chubby throat swelled and shivered with mawkish sincerity.

His mother sang it faster, sweeter, better; but how long ago? It was the song she sang at his uncle's wedding when he was five or six, with the one, two, three, one, two, three um-pah of a band behind her. She sang at parties, social clubs, and weddings, always at his father's request.

When the song was over Ian looked up to see Jennah standing beside the couch, a glass of wine in each hand, one offered toward him with a slightly baffled expression. Ian gripped Peter too tightly, and he woke squinting, puzzled by sleep. Sitting up and stretching, he asked what was wrong, and Ian said that it was nothing, just a song. A stupid song he hadn't heard in years.

Peter lit a fire in his room, a small coal fire, and they sat beside each other in front of the hearth watching the coals slowly catch. Their shadows joined and stuttered over the bed as the room gradually warmed, and they agreed that this, a real open fire, was a luxury. Ian could remember the change from having a coal fire to gas central heating at his parents' house. Closing the chimney and installing a new gas heater meant an end to the lingering colds and chest infections that marked his early childhood. It was a vague memory, perhaps even one of his mother's stories, something that he did not directly remember.

Peter asked what he was thinking.

'Nothing much.' Ian slowly shook his head. 'I was remembering my parents' house. We always had a fire going, sometimes through the summer, depending on the weather. They worried about my chest. It used to be a problem because I wasn't very active, and if I got a cold it would immediately go to my chest. For as long as I can remember my parents checked on me every night to make sure I was sleeping on my left side. It was a good feeling knowing that they would do that, watch out for you.' Ian shifted back from the fire a little.

'You forget these things when you're healthy. Some of it only makes sense when you're older.'

Peter asked what he meant.

'When Gordon moved to his grandmother's, he spent most of his time with us. I told you about that?'

Peter nodded.

'He stayed over most nights when Mrs Marshall was working. We used to share a bed, and it only just occurred to me that my parents didn't have to check on me any more. I was probably more active when Gordon was around. I remember being healthier. But I think the main reason for having Gordon stay was so that he would look out for me.' Ian breathed out slowly, watching the flames fold softly around the pressed pieces of coal.

Ian began to undress. Peter asked if he was alright, and Ian said yes, but shook his head, his eyes dry from staring into the coals. He was, he thought, giving too much of himself away.

Helping him undress, Peter pulled Ian's sweater free of his head.

Ian looked up from the fire. 'I was adopted,' he said. 'I was taken into care at eleven months.' He spoke quickly, his voice flat, matter of fact. 'My birth mother brought me to the hospital with my arm tugged out at the shoulder. The joint was popped right out of the socket and it was left untreated for a number of days. Long enough to fuck it up. If she'd done something about it sooner then everything would have sorted itself out.'

Peter drew Ian's shirt over his shoulders and asked if he was serious. He was talking, he said, as if it were a story, as if it had happened to someone else.

Ian stood in front of the fire, heat pressing against his legs, and unbuttoning his jeans he explained that what he knew was not even much of a story, as he didn't know any of the details. It sounded dramatic, but in reality it was much more banal.

'Do you know who your real mother is?'

'My birth mother?' Ian shook his head. 'I know her last name was Cullom.'

'And she was responsible?'

'For my arm?'

Peter nodded.

'She was prosecuted so there are court and police records. She was young. I used to think that my adopted father was my real father. I knew it wasn't true. I don't know why I thought it.' This was, he said, ending the conversation, as much as he knew.

Ian woke in the night, confused, believing that he was back at Gordon's. Peter slept with his knees tucked into Ian's knees, and his arm resting over Ian's side. Ian felt that he was being held down. The fire burned hot, flushing the walls red, and the coals hummed and cracked. Ian twisted on to his back, and Peter rolled beside him gently holding his right hand, interlocking their fingers. Physically confused, Ian slipped back into sleep, and for one brief moment he thought that Gordon was in the room, sitting in a chair beside the door, the firelight catching his face, watching with his arms folded, disapproving. Jolting, he woke properly, unsure if it was Gordon or Terry that he dreamed of, shocked at the idea that either one of them could see him. Waking, Peter chuckled and coughed, half-asleep himself, and drew the quilt close around them.

Ian leaned back into Peter's arms and tightly closed his eyes, counting up and down in a soothing rhythm as the fire spat and sang, animating the room. One, and-and-and; two, and-and-and; three, and-and-and; two, and-and-and; one, and-and-and.

They agreed to arrive at work separately, wanting to keep themselves private, but they cycled in together nevertheless and arrived at Endell Street sullen and sulky, the weekend already behind them. As they locked their bikes they checked to see if there was anyone around who might recognize them. For the first time Ian felt that being a messenger was work, real work, something he might resent.

Curt and irritable, Dom told them that they were two riders short, and Mondays being what they are, they were likely to be busy. Derek sat beside the desk with a newspaper open on his lap.

Ian thought about Peter the whole day through. Sometimes wanting to see him, and sometimes wondering what this sudden hankering was. Whatever it was he indulged himself, comparing people to Peter throughout the day, looking for familiarities in pedestrians on the street, secretaries giving and taking packages, harassed lawyers and publicists. He was wearing a sweater borrowed from Peter, and caught in the wool was the faint cold reek of the coal fire. Waiting between pick-ups, Ian breathed deeply into the cuff, recalling small and private details of the weekend.

They decided to eat in Covent Garden after work. Jennah would not be home until late, and once again neither of them wanted to cook.

The day was slower than Dom had hoped for, and cold. Ian managed eighteen pick-ups, and Peter twenty-nine.

Peter said his wrist hurt, he'd jolted it cycling off the pavement. Standing in the doorway for Western Messengers, he rolled up his sleeve and wrapped a support bandage around his hand and forearm, telling again the story of the man tumbling down the stairs on top of him. Ian asked if he was alright, and holding up his hand to show him, Peter said yes. It wasn't anything out of the ordinary.

Locking their bikes together on Endell Street, they walked to Covent Garden to find the streets thick with people. Traffic backed through the side streets, blocking the length of Long Acre, and people loitered between stopped cars, looking west to St. Martin's Lane. Puzzled, Peter glanced back up Endell Street. Somebody, he said, was shouting Ian's name. Ian stopped to listen but heard nothing rise above the bustle on the street.

The road beside the tube station was so crowded that the hawkers and performers were pushed back to the shop windows. Commuters waited in the entrance to the Underground. At the end of Floral Street there were two fire engines and a great number of uniformed police with hard helmets and fluorescent jackets. Despite the crowd and the police and the stalled traffic, everything seemed calm. The incident, whatever it was, was not urgent.

Waiting outside Bakers in Bedford Court, Peter rested his hand on Ian's shoulder as they decided on pies and beers, and whether one or the other should go and buy cigarettes. People stood in a jumble blocking the pavement, and behind them a couple discussed the crowd, saying that Leicester Square was cordoned off and packed with police and firemen. The Underground also was not running. It was, they thought, either a fire or a bomb in one of the cinemas or one of the bars behind the cinemas. More likely than not it was a bomb threat, as there were a number of ambulances and, as yet, no smoke. A small commotion, some shouting, some horse-play, rustled through the crowd from Covent Garden.

Uncomfortable, Peter said that they should return home, and find something on their way back. Smelling some kind of astringent or chemical cleaner, Ian turned, holding his breath. Immediately behind them stood two men in oil-stained bomber jackets and blue knitted hats. Breathing out, he whispered, *one*.

Grabbing Ian by the collar the first man kicked his feet from under him, forcing him first to his knees, then down to his side. The crowd shied back, pushing against the cars trapped in the street, as the man hiked Ian's sweater over his head. Dragging him backward along the pavement, the man rolled

Ian into the gutter, leaving him flailing and wrestling with his clothes. With an open can of paintstripper in one hand, the second man punched Peter hard across his ear, knocking him down to his hands and knees. Kicking Peter on to his back, the man held the canister over Peter's head and shook it like a bottle of sauce. The crowd fled further back. Peter curled tightly on to his side, hollering, his hands locked over his face before the first gobbets spattered his arms. There was a hoarse shout of 'police!' and the two thugs bolted into the crowd.

Ian struggled to his feet and with one shoe gone, he hobbled to Peter's side. Peter tugged frantically at his clothes, holding them away from his skin, and shrieking through clenched teeth. The man had punched him with keys gripped in his fist, splitting his earlobe. Falling beside him, Ian wiped the paintstripper from his stomach with his bare hand, shouting that they needed help.

People stood in the restaurant, pointing through the window, astonished. The crowd closed about them and Ian was quickly pulled up and off and hurried through the restaurant to the kitchen. His hand was slippy, numb and rubbery from the acid. Looking back, he shouted for Peter, his voice coarse and breaking.

The police arrived and Peter was carried directly to the kitchen, lifted shoulder-high, bucking and coughing, feet first, doors bursting open. Ian stood shirtless at the sink, his hand held under running water, the water pink with crimson dye burned out from Peter's sweater. Seeing Peter lumbered across the kitchen Ian tried to go to him, but two men held him back, forcing his hand under the tap. There was no sensation in his fingers and his wrist was rashed red. Metal filings added to the stripper caught and cut into his hand, reopening the grazes on his fingertips.

Peter stood naked in a huge bath-like sink, shivering and coughing as he was hosed with cold water, his hands gripped around his head, the support bandage unspooled from his wrist, and his bare scuffed knees level with everyone's chins. On his chest was a broad and sore blotch where the stripper had soaked through his sweater and burned him.

Uncooked pies were set on trays stacked beside the ovens; the kitchen staff stood as a group by the double doors. Ian attempted a second time to pull away from the water. Told to stay where he was, he began to count out loud in a rapid tom-tom rhythm – one, two two two; one, two two two – concentrating on his hand. A waiter brought him a bowl filled with ice and water, and they sat him down with the bowl on his lap. As the doors swung open customers rose again, wanting to see what was happening.

The manager calmly organized the kitchen staff, ordering them back to their stations, when from the back of the kitchen came a clatter of cutlery and pans skittering across the floor. Ian cowered, ducking over the bowl, certain that the two men had returned. Embarrassed, one of the kitchen staff raised his hands and explained that he'd knocked over a tray, nothing else; he'd walked into a tray and knocked it on the floor.

Except for the rush of water and Ian's counting, the kitchen became silent, filled with the sickly stink of raw ground meat.

The police walked Ian and Peter out through the back doors to a squad car. The streets were blocked and an ambulance could not come through, even from Leicester Square. One of the policemen carried their sodden clothes and shoes in a plastic bag.

The officer made sure that Ian was sitting back properly when he closed the door. As the car reversed into the road, people pointed at them. Ian shook his hand, easing the sting. Wrapped in towels, Peter shivered violently, and his ear bled steadily, soaking the towel. As more people gathered around the car he buried his face between his knees.

*

Ian sat on a long examination table in a small square curtained booth with his hand held up in front of him, greased with a thick and numbing salve. He worried that the thugs would return. The two policemen waited with Peter, and Ian wanted to ask one of them to stay in view, but the curtain would not fully close and it was humiliating enough to sit in the room, cold, half-naked, within feet of a busy public corridor. Jennah argued with the police, demanding to know what was being done to catch the men responsible for the attack. Ian listened as one of the officers calmly answered her questions, knowing that Jennah would ask him the same questions and he would not know what to say.

Jennah came to the booth, and standing at the opening she held out her mobile phone and asked if there was someone she could call for him. Ian shook his head and managing to clear his throat he asked after Peter. Jennah curtly nodded and cocked her head to one side. The doctors, she said, were stitching his ear.

'Is he alright?'

She nodded again, a short single nod, refusing details, and stepped into the booth. Peter, she said, would not talk to her. So what did Ian have to say? 'Do you know why this happened?'

Ian thought of the man's face, sharp and weasel-like. The memory brought the stink of paintstripper back into the room, vivid and noxious.

'I have to keep my hand up. It hurts less.'

'This was deliberate, wasn't it?'

Ian shook his head, and said that none of it made sense. There was no logic to the attack.

'Was Peter being affectionate?'

Ian thought back to the very moment before the assault, but there was nothing of consequence to recall.

'Why did they only attack Peter?'

Ian said that he did not know. 'The whole thing happened so quick. One of them grabbed me.'

'But he didn't hurt you.'

Ian could not reply.

'This was deliberate.' Her tone was accusatory. 'Why only Peter? You don't carry a can of paintstripper around on a whim.'

He did not want to consider this question. Tapping his heels together, he wished that she would disappear.

'Their actions were categorical,' she insisted. 'Why did they do this?' The men were organized, she said, prepared, they knew what they were doing. This was not opportunistic or casual. Their intention, she said, was to assault Peter.

This was, she did not doubt, a reprisal.

Jennah guided her brother to her car, whispering so that Ian could not hear her. Peter did not reply, and Ian followed behind, his hand bandaged cartoon-like and freakishly huge. Parked under the Emergency awning, Jennah's car blocked the way for ambulances. As they approached a man hurried from the front passenger seat and opened the rear passenger door.

They sat waiting for the traffic to clear, the radio tuned to the police channel, reports of a bomb threat but no bomb. Peter huddled on the seat beside Ian, his head tucked between his knees, refusing to talk. His sister reached across from the front passenger seat, and stroking his hair cooed to him, ignoring Ian and her companion.

Back at Hunter's Close Jennah put her brother to bed. Ian sat at the dining table shaking his hand trying to stave off an irritating prickling. Although numb, his fingertips itched. Jennah's partner busied himself brewing a pot of real coffee, then sitting opposite Ian, he repeatedly cleaned his glasses.

Ian stood up when Jennah came downstairs. Wiping her hands together, she looked harshly at him, full of blame.

'He won't talk to me. I'll make him something, and you can

take it up. Maybe he will talk to you.' The police were coming, she said, checking her watch, they would arrive in an hour.

Ian asked what more the police could want. Jennah said that she didn't know, but rather than keeping them at the hospital the police had agreed to come to the house. 'And then I'll take you home.'

Ian stood beside Jennah as she waited for the kettle. He was unwelcome now, and in the absence of a rational explanation for the assault he would have to shoulder the blame. The fresh coffee sat out ignored as Jennah prepared a cup of instant coffee, opening the lid, spooning out the granules, replacing the lid, brisk and angry. She clearly did not want him in the house. Whatever his disagreement with Gordon, Ian was confident that he could return to the Grove.

Ian said again that he knew nothing about the attack. The only sign that something was wrong was the smell of paintstripper, and by the time he could smell it, the men were upon them.

Jennah watched the kettle boil. 'It wasn't ordinary paintstripper. They used a chemical cleaner. You can't buy it off the shelf.'

Ian caught their reflections in the kitchen window. The three of them looked hollow and exhausted, their eye-sockets black and empty. Jennah poured the hot water into Peter's cup. Then looking at Ian's hand she realized that he would not be able to carry it. Pouring the coffee away, she told him to go upstairs.

Peter lay on his side facing the wall. Still messy from Sunday's breakfast, the room reeked of curry spice, fat, and garlic. Foil cartons were strewn across the floor, food thickened inside. Peter flinched as Ian leant over him, attempting to look into his face. There was a swelling on his cheek, a perfectly round bruise, and a ragged scratch that ran across his temple. Hair pressed into the tape that held the bandage over his ear. On the cabinet next to the lube and condoms were three medicine bottles from the bathroom.

Ian stumbled around the room trying to tidy away the plates, but the bandage on his hand prevented him from picking them up.

He scuffed them carefully together, making a small pile in front of the fire; the grate was cold and full, ash spilled on to the hearth.

Peter cleared his throat. The man who assaulted him had said Ian's name. 'He knew your name.'

Confused, Ian came closer to the bed.

Peter was dozy with the medication, lucid but slow. Turning carefully on to his back, he drew down the bed-sheet. The burn on his chest was as large as a handprint. The raw skin was greasy with salve and pricked with small white blisters. Ian could not look.

'He said your name.'

Ian did not understand. Peter impatiently closed his eyes. Ian Cullom. 'He knew your name. Cullom. Ian Cullom.'

Knocking on the door, Jennah said that the police were here.

They sat in Jennah's office, two police officers and Ian crowded into the one small room. One policeman sat beside the door on a stool brought up from the kitchen, and the other, a woman, sat facing Ian. There were doors on the cupboards, and locks on the doors. Books, folders, pens, and papers, tidied away. Beside the computer a modem flashed, still connected. The officer asked Ian how he was, and Ian automatically replied that he was alright.

'This shouldn't,' she promised, 'take very long.' There was concern in the officer's voice, and she sat with her hands together, holding a small notebook open on her lap. After talking with Peter, she had questions, she said, but it would be better if Ian told her everything in his own words. 'But first,' she asked, 'if you could tell me where you live?'

Ian hesitated before answering. Standing back from the door, Jennah waited in the corridor, listening with her arms folded.

'I'm staying with a friend in Camberwell.'

'Can you give me the address?'

Ian could not remember the street name or the house number. Instead he clumsily described the house and named the streets on either side, becoming more and more anxious until he remembered that it was Vicarage Grove. Number seventeen.

'And you work as a courier?'

Ian nodded yes, and the officer nodded with him.

The officer asked Ian to describe the attack, and as he spoke she checked the details, slowly drawing him back to the event. Ian described the walk from Western to Porters, recalling their conversation, the crowd, and the sudden appearance of the two men. Even with the officer's interruptions there was little to tell. The man that attacked him was wearing black jeans and a dirty black bomber jacket with frayed cuffs and collar. Both were spotted with oil and paint and dirt. His boots were workmen's boots, light brown, chaffed, old. Under his jacket was a blue T-shirt. It was harder to describe his face. Ian doubted that he would recognize the man if he saw him again.

Leaning forward, the officer asked about the name Ian Cullom. Behind her Jennah stepped up to the open door.

Ian shook his head. 'It's not my proper name. My surname is Proctor.'

The woman nodded. 'If it isn't your name, why would anyone use it?'

'I used to live in a squat, and I used the name on a travel pass. I needed the pass to open an electricity account.'

'Who else knew the name?'

'The other people in the squat. Louise and Malc.'

Writing down their names, the officer asked if they also lived at Vicarage Grove.

Ian shook his head. 'We lived in a squat in Hopewell Terrace.

I don't know where Louise is now. I think she's gone back to her parents, somewhere in Surrey. Malc just came out of hospital, and I don't know where he is either. He might be living with his brother in New Cross.'

'Is there anyone else who would know you by that name?'

Ian shrugged. 'Terry. Terrance Noxley. Malc's brother. He was always at the squat. It's possible that he would know.'

'Is there any reason why he or anyone else would want to do this?'

Ian shook his head.

'No reason you can think of?'

'No. Nothing I can think of.'

Dissatisfied, the officer repeated her questions. Growing more and more uncomfortable, Ian repeated his answers, determined to leave as soon as possible. Jennah stood at the door, arms tightly folded and an expression of disgust and anger set on her face. She also, he guessed, wanted him gone.

Gordon's front door was bolted from the inside. Waiting for the taxi to back its way down the street, Ian turned his key uselessly in the lock, listening to the latch turn. He stood back from the front steps and shouted up, waited then shouted again, but nothing stirred in the house. It was the last day of the month, Gordon should be home. The car was also gone.

The lane behind Gordon's was littered with paper, and as he reached the gate he recognized the clothes hanging from the trees at the back of the yard. Gordon's shirts, trousers, and sweaters hung limp and sopping from the bare black branches. Books and papers flung from the second-storey windows were scattered over the lawn and path, all sodden with the weekend's rain.

Gordon's mattress and blankets slumped on the paving beside the house, underneath them the cooker was collapsed on its side. Squinting into the night, Ian looked at the clutter, imagining the flurry of papers scattering down, and the heavier plummet of the cooker, and mattress.

The back door was unlocked, and he stepped cautiously into the house, holding protectively to the banisters, eyes adjusting to the darkness, ears adjusting to the silence. Down from a pillow or quilt lay in small white drifts in the corners of the stairs. The walls were gouged and scratched with a rough zippered line. Ian called up for Gordon, and the cat panicked at the top of the stairs. Scurrying into the kitchen, she answered with a long lowing mewl.

Ian clucked his tongue to soothe and coax the cat, aware of a terrible and familiar chemical smell. Reaching the upper landing he stopped and waited, taking stock of the damage. The floor was drecked with broken glass and crockery. Slyly backing under upturned boxes, the cat hissed at him, hackles up, fur thick with down.

Ian checked the house room by room, and found them more or less empty. Jammed up against the sitting-room door, the settee was slashed and gutted, its back and covers slit open. Gordon's television and CD player were missing.

The bedroom was the hub of the tumult, the walls were doused with paintstripper. Paint and paper wilted in soft and baggy folds. Gordon's quilt and pillows were split open, and a mat of feathers coated the floor. Returning to the hall, Ian checked the bathroom, his eyes beginning to sting and water.

Torn in half, with the cover ripped off, Gordon's ledger and a wad of papers were stuffed into the toilet. Unwrapping the bandage from his hand, Ian picked out the wet paper and carbons and lay them one on top of the other, pressing them dry between sheets of toilet paper. Except for a list of Patterson's properties, most of the pages were blank. Carefully rolling them up, he tucked them into his pocket, and wrapped the bandage back over his hand. This was, he didn't doubt, Terry's doing. The ripped ledger, the wrecked house. It was possible that

Terry held Gordon responsible for his arrest. Although Ian did not understand why.

Ian called Gordon's mobile and after two rings the phone was answered. Recognizing Shannon's voice, he asked for Gordon. Shannon quickly replied that Gordon was up in Kettering, working. Who was this?

Ian asked if she had seen Malc or Terry, and recognizing his voice, Shannon said no. Gordon was in Kettering, and if Ian had any sense he should leave also, lay low and stay out of the way. Had she heard anything from Gordon? Anything at all? Shannon said no, other people were looking for him, and when Ian asked who they were, she paused and said that she did not know.

Ian explained that he was leaving town tomorrow, could he see her tonight? 'I know he isn't in Kettering.'

Shannon would not answer her door. Knocking harder, Ian called through the letterbox. Coming out of the bedroom, Shannon switched on the hall light and wrapped herself in a man's dressing gown, her gestures impatient and testy. Ian watched through the mottled glass and could not stop himself knocking one more time. The cat stirred under his coat. Opening the door, Shannon made no attempt to disguise her irritation. Returning into the house to close her bedroom door, she told him not to come inside. What are you doing coming here, she asked, it's the middle of the night.

Beside the door was a suitcase. 'I told you earlier I don't know where Gordon is.'

'You said he was in Kettering. I know he isn't there.'

They both looked at the suitcase.

'I have a friend staying.' With her white hair tied back tight and flat, Shannon looked smaller than she was, and frailer. Ian doubted that there was anyone else in the house. 'You can't stay.' She paused and looked properly at him for the first time, noticing his bandaged hand. 'Ian, you have to go. I have no idea where Gordon is.'

'He always tells someone where he's going. Always.'

Telling him that she could not help, Shannon closed the door.

Watching her through the rutted glass Ian knocked as hard as he could using the back of his bandaged hand. Leaning against the door, Shannon waited for him to leave. Her hair, face, and skinny arms fuzzed white and ghostly under the hallway light. Ian stopped knocking, and for some moments neither of them moved. Then, with a gesture of frustration, Shannon opened the door and ushered him in, telling him that he could have the couch or the floor, but she didn't have any blankets.

'I want you out first thing. You aren't stopping here.'

As Ian stepped into the hall the cat yowled from inside his coat. Unbuttoning the coat, he let the cat struggle out.

Shannon hurried ahead into the lounge, attempting to close the door before the cat slipped through. 'She can't stay. I can't have a cat.'

'You can take her to Gordon tomorrow.'

'I've no idea where he is.' Shannon kneeled beside the couch, searching for the cat.

'When did you last see him?'

Shannon settled back on her haunches, now clearly angry. 'I saw him on Sunday. Sunday evening. He said he was going to Kettering.'

'What for?'

'He didn't say.' She shook her head.

'Does he know about his house?'

Shannon closed her eyes, giving the faintest nod. 'It happened on Sunday. He wasn't there.'

'And why do you have his phone?'

Exhausted, Shannon closed her eyes again. One hand held the dressing gown. 'I've told you everything I know. I don't know anything else. I want you out before I'm up. I don't want anyone to know that you were here.'

Ian sat up until dawn writing a letter to Gordon, using the damp blank paper torn from the ledger. When the letter was finished he screwed the paper into a ball. He carefully crept into the hall, and checked the side pockets on the suitcase, suspecting that Shannon either intended to join Gordon, wherever he was, or would otherwise be seeing him. He found nothing in the small side pockets, and nothing in either the kitchen or lounge that told him of her plans.

With the room brightening Ian settled on the couch, but he could not get comfortable. Pulling the cushions on to the floor he lay on them, but he still could not settle. The cat watched with wide eyes and an occasional growl from under an armchair. He scratched at the carpet, hoping to lure her out, but secure in the corner she stayed where she was. The cat would have starved, he thought, she has no gratitude. She has no trust, he corrected himself.

Ian sat up waiting for Shannon. Listening to her move around her bedroom, he felt that she was waiting for him to leave the house, postponing the moment that she would have to talk with him. Coming out already dressed, she stood at the sitting-room door, her face made up, looking formal and determined, and asked what he was still doing here? Ian said nothing and waited while she picked up after herself. Checking windows, throwing out contents from the fridge, and taking out the rubbish, she was obviously leaving.

'What are you going to do about the cat?'

'I told you, she can't stay here.'

Checking her watch, Shannon told Ian that he would have to leave. Now. He asked about the cat again, and in frustration she said that she could ask someone to come and feed it or take it away.

'She needs a litter tray. She needs food.'

'I know.'

'So, you're going then?' Ian stood up. He would leave the house, let her believe that she was rid of him.

Ian waited for Shannon by the bins, checking first that there was nobody waiting for him, lurking in the stairwell or forecourt. The day was bright and clear and crisp, cold enough for Ian to see his breath. Children sat on the steps, dressed and ready for school. Watching the balcony he saw Shannon come out of the flat. Double-locking the door she walked two doors up to give keys and money to her neighbour. Pointing back to her flat she talked briefly with a man in a vest, his hair scraggy, his gestures slow and sleepy. Ian watched the stairs, waiting for her to come down. She saw him the moment she stepped out into the forecourt.

'What are you waiting for?'

'I thought I'd see you off.'

'You can leave me alone, that's what you can do.'

She walked quickly. The bag was heavy and she lumbered it against her hip.

'I could carry it for you.'

'Do you want me to shout?' Shannon set the suitcase down. Now very frustrated. 'Look. I let you stay last night. I put you up. Now fuck off. I don't want anyone to see me with you.'

'Who don't you want me to see? The people who did this?' Ian held up his hand.

Shannon looked up to the sky and groaned, her voice edged with desperation. 'For Christ-sakes Ian. All you're doing is making more trouble. You'll make this worse.'

Ian picked up her suitcase. 'What are you taking? The bus or the train?'

Shannon stayed where she was. Giving up, she walked after him. Keeping several steps behind.

*

They stood apart at the bus stop. Shannon smoking, and Ian keeping her suitcase between his feet. When the bus came, Ian hauled the suitcase on board, and they stood together at the back, close to the stairs and the open platform. Ian's hand was starting to throb.

'Where are you meeting him?'

Shannon turned away. Other passengers squinted out at the road and the traffic, minds elsewhere. At the front of the bus was a small poster with the two sketchy drawings of the men who had assaulted Sumpter. There was a reward for information, and a freephone number.

'Who are you staying with?'

'I'm going to see my parents.'

Ian unwrapped the bandage on his hand, and holding it out, described the assault. Shannon looked sideways at his hand then out of the window. Other passengers turned to look at his hand. Caught in the traffic, the bus stopped at New Cross Gate station. A man in an orange jacket cut the flowers and papers away from the railings at the bridge, and people passed without noticing as the dead and plastic flowers and wreaths were thrown away. Holding his hand to Shannon's face, Ian repeated that they had thrown acid on Peter. Acid. In a crowded street, in the middle of London.

Pursing her lips, Shannon stared hard out of the window, her grey eyes narrowed. 'Terry was working the benefits. He had someone change the names and addresses at Hastings Road.'

'Malc?'

Shaking her head, Shannon turned fully around. 'It wasn't Malc. I think it was the boy that was thrown from the bus.'

'Sumpter?'

Shannon nodded and looked cautiously at the other passengers. Leaning closer to him she spoke in a low clear voice. 'Terry and Gordon came to the club one night. Terry said he had money coming to him. A lot of money, and he was bragging about what he'd done. He didn't say who it was, but it definitely wasn't Malc. Malc might have given him the idea, but, as far as I know, he wouldn't have anything to do with it.'

'When was this? Before the assault?'

Shannon said yes. She couldn't remember exactly. It was a couple of months ago. 'The money never came through. Gordon said it hadn't worked and that's why what happened to that boy happened.'

'Why didn't you go to the police?'

Shannon looked down at Ian's hand. The fingers were rutted with soft dead skin, a little fat, white, and swollen.

'Was Gordon involved?'

'If he was, it was only to let Terry use the houses.'

'But he knew about Sumpter?'

'It was too much of a coincidence not to be him.'

'Did he tell you he wasn't involved?'

'Something like that.'

'Because you wanted to hear it, or because it was true?'

'Would it make any difference?' She shook her head again.

'He wouldn't run unless he'd done something.'

More people climbed on to the bus and they pushed further up the aisle, standing close, almost touching. Moving forward again, Shannon looked at the other passengers. They were in Camberwell now, just past Vicarage Grove.

'Why didn't anyone go to the police?'

'And tell them what? The police already had a list of the names that Terry used. How much more did they need?'

'What if there wasn't any list?'

'But there was.'

'What if it wasn't enough?'

Shannon shrugged.

'I don't understand how any of you could sit by, knowing what you knew, and not do anything.'

'It might not be true. We didn't have any proof.'

'What proof did you need?'

Shannon looked sharply at him with quick and bitter reproach. 'None of this has anything to do with me.'

Ian turned away. He felt sick, physically ill. His mouth suddenly dry and his stomach tight. Shannon's story was more repugnant than he could have imagined.

They sat in the waiting room at Victoria Coach Station. Ian watched the buses out on the concourse, and Shannon sat in the bay window, watching the doors, with the morning sun on her back, and a cup of black coffee on the table in front of her.

Ian wiped the table with his sleeve.

'Gordon was involved. Why else would he have left?'

'He thought he was protecting you.'

'I don't need looking after.'

'Your friend,' she asked. 'Did they hurt him?'

Ian nodded.

'Badly?'

'Bad enough for him not to see me again.'

'Maybe you should call.'

Ian shook his head. 'I think it was supposed to be me. Peter had a bandage on his arm. But I'm not sure they were that particular which one of us they picked.' Sitting up, Ian coughed. What he didn't understand, he said, was how Terry managed to find people to do this when he was already in police custody?

Shannon said she didn't doubt that he had. Turning her chair sideways, she looked out of the window.

'What are you going to do?' she asked.

'About Gordon? I don't know. It's hard to know. He's always looked after me.' Ian counted the passengers queuing for the buses. 'What about you?'

'I'm going to Paris in two weeks, and then Hamburg. I have an agent now. I'll be working through the summer. I can't have any trouble.'

'You'll do well.'

'I'll do something.'

After seeing Shannon off, Ian walked back to Victoria Station unclear about what he should do. Inside the station was a row of telephones with small perspex hoods. Up on the boards Ian saw signs for Hastings and he thought that he should call his father. Pasted under one of the hoods were numbers for a police helpline.

It was possible that Shannon was wrong. It was possible that Terry had done nothing more than a modest scam, signing on under other names, without his brother's or Sumpter's aid. But the alternative was appalling. It was possible, it was likely, that Terry arranged the attack on Sumpter. Taking out the list of names from his wallet, Ian unfolded the paper, and calling the helpline he waited for the answering service. When the recording started he described the scam, gave as much information as he knew, then finally read out the names. Michael Alton, Donald Anderson, Malcolm Andrews, Ian Butcher, Robert Clark, Matthew Forest, Lee Gordon, Alan Hudson, David Jones, Andrew King, Terrance Kelman, Robert Latchford, David Lawson, Henry Lewis, Simon McDonald, Duncan McGregor, Jim McKenzie, John Peterson, James Pearson, Steven Seargent, David Smallford, Christopher Smith, Dennis Taylor, Simon Thomas, David Williams, Peter Wittle, William Young.

Stepping out on to the concourse he looked up at the glass roof, grateful for the sunlight, watching pigeons panic and settle. Dirtier than rats, he thought, grubby, stupid, and scrawny.

Ian walked down Hopewell Terrace. The first set of houses was completed, and as he looked through the windows he could not imagine himself inside.

The streetlights cut across lacquered wood floors and bare pink plaster walls. The rooms were deep, and configured differently in each house; bare brick fireplaces built with plain and wide slate hearths. Ian could smell paint. There was rain coming.

The boards were removed from the windows of number 7, and he climbed over the windowledge and into the house without trouble. There was still work to be done. The interior was marked out, and new floorboards were stacked along the joists, a basic shape restored to the house by slender steel posts, outlining the walls. There was less that was familiar to him, and he stepped across the joists thinking that none of them might have lived there, and that in two short weeks a small part of the house's history was easily erased. New pipes and conduits ran under the floors. Standing motionless in the heart of the house he stared into the darkness, concentrating on the black playing field, fingering the money in his pocket. The notes were new and crisp, everything he owned in one pocket. Bounded by a damp blackness, he asked himself what he was doing coming back to Hopewell.

Out in the field a fox wove back and forth, skulking closer, unseen and silent towards the house. Stopping in mid-path it began to bark and holler.

Catching sight of her, Ian began to count between the calls. One-two, one-two. She could smell him, he was sure. His eyes shifted and the fox dissolved. Hugging his arm Ian counted a soft and slow, one-two, one-two, one-two, listening.